Don't
Cosplay
with My
Heart

Don't Cosplay with My Heart

Cecil Castellucci

SCHOLASTIC PRESS

NEW YORK

Text copyright © 2018 by Cecil Castellucci
Illustrations copyright © 2018 by Marcelo Baez
Additional interior imagery: © veleo5/Shutterstock and cajoer/Thinkstock

Library of Congress Cataloging-in-Publication Data available

ISBN 978-1-338-12549-8
10 9 8 7 6 5 4 3 2 1   18 19 20 21 22

Printed in the U.S.A.   23
First edition, January 2018
Book design by Elizabeth Parisi

To the boy in comics I like the most.
Which when I wrote this book was you.

Summer

ANGELES COMIC CON

One

It's no wonder when I see the cheap Gargantua mask I picked up on Free Comic Book Day this past spring on my desk, I put it on and leave it on when I am called down to dinner. Gargantua, my favorite character from Team Tomorrow, is ten feet tall and so is the size of my being pissed off at everything right now.

"Take that mask off, Edan," my dad says when he sees me.

"No," I say. "You can't force me to."

I make myself comfortable at the table. I feel indestructible. He cannot say anything to me with any authority.

"Edan. It is impossible to eat with that on," he says.

"No, it's not, see." I shove the fork into my mouth and chew big and exaggerated. Truth be told, the plastic does cut into the side of my face a little, and it's a bit hard to chew, but not enough to make eating *impossible*.

Nothing is impossible for Gargantua. You don't have to have read every Team Tomorrow comic book to know that.

Right now in my heart, it is like a classic superhero battle between good and evil. It is every feeling all at once run amok. I could go down either path.

"Let Edan be," my mom says quietly.

"This is one of my last dinners with my family, Mel," my dad says. "I want it to be nice."

No matter how delicious the food is in front of us, no matter how many candles are lit, this is not going to be a nice dinner at all.

The past few months, there have been quiet rumbles in the family. My dad has been different. *Cagey.* It started with fights with my mom behind closed doors. Then there were late-night sneak-outs for meetings at the office and worried long phone calls at strange hours. And now it's all come out. "There's an inquiry at the corporate head office," he explains, and Dad has to be *sequestered.*

"You shouldn't have gotten involved with this mess," my mom's voice warbles.

My dad is with a company that deals with payroll for Hollywood productions, and from what I can understand from all of his recent overexplaining and question dodging about the situation we're in, some of the money meant for one place went to pay for another place and some of the money didn't get to where it was supposed to end up at all. And now that it's been discovered, he's the one left holding the bag.

"Why aren't Mark and Bobby and Lawrence and Tyler part of the inquiry?" Her voice may be cracking into a million pieces, but she slams the table with her hands with the force of a person wielding superhuman strength when she asks the question. It startles everyone because it is so unexpected.

"You have to understand the corporate structure," Dad says, trying to mansplain things to her. "There's a hierarchy. The team has a plan for how this is going to roll out. I'm going first."

My mother snorts.

"I was a senior VP at a production company once upon a time," she says. "I know how these things go."

Mom pushes her full plate away from her.

"I just can't," Mom says, and then it's as though all of a sudden the fight she had in her just winks away.

I adjust my Gargantua mask and then push my plate away in solidarity.

"May I be excused?" I ask, even though everyone here at this table knows that no one needs permission to do anything anymore. I cannot get into trouble, because whatever he's allegedly done is way worse than anything that I've ever done or likely will ever do.

Unless I go totally rogue like Gargantua did when she was betrayed.

She was one of the original members of the team until she left and changed from good to bad and then back to good-ish again.

Gargantua was fierce and did terrible things when she turned against the team. But can you blame her? When they fought their enemy, Split Second in the Time War, a choice was made by Team Tomorrow to save the area where New Big City would one day be from winking out of time. It was a cold calculation meant to cause minimum damage to the team, but the result was that Gargantua's whole history was wiped out of time. The team tricked her into sacrificing her past so they could save the future. It was for the greater good, but it devastated her and altered her view of the world.

Gargantua went rogue and systematically destroyed the life of one of her former team members' relatives in revenge.

But of course, that just left her hollow. Most people will go along with anything to keep their past and keep their friends. Maybe that's why Dad was acting like it was all going to be all right. Maybe it's easier.

Instead, Gargantua became a woman without a past and without friends. But that was only until they rebooted the team and started back at issue 1. In comics, the stories always change.

My dad looks from Mom to me, and back to her again. He shakes his head from side to side sadly. He doesn't even try to use his charming smile on us.

There is only raw truth served up at this table now. And it's pretty ugly.

"Do what you want," he sighs. He knows he's lost this round.

My mom and I both quit the table, leaving him looking small and crumpled as he sits alone.

Mom goes to bed, even though it's only 7:00 p.m.

I head to the family room to play video games. Only exploring fantastical realms and destroying evil aliens can get me through the night. This time while I'm playing the game, I do something that I never do. I make all the *bad* choices. The ones that get me totally into the personality red rather than the blue. I am evil.

It feels really good to not follow my regular path.

Maybe it's the Gargantua mask that makes me bolder in my game-playing choices.

The most interesting thing I notice is that all these parts of the story I had never seen before in this game, my third play through, open up. It is as though I am playing a whole new game and becoming a whole new me.

Maybe I need to be her more and me less.

This kills a few hours, which feels good, but I still have the whole summer to save. Usually, we go on some family trip somewhere. But now that my father will be away, this summer is different, and we're going nowhere and everything feels hard. Not as hard as losing your past hard. Not as hard as going through something totally horrifying hard. Just emotionally hard.

I power down the game and go to my room and try to figure out how to save my summer. That's what Gargantua would do. She is self-rescuing.

"Make your own fun," I say, repeating the mantra that my best friend, Kasumi, always says. I wish she was here and not in Japan for the summer. "Make your own fun," I say again, flipping on my tablet and surfing the net.

I search for things to do for free (or nearly) in Los Angeles in summer.

"Boring. Boring. Boring. Boring."

I reject one thing and then another and then another.

"There is no fun!" I bellow to the action figures and Funko dolls that live stuffed to the brim on the shelf in the corner of my room.

That's when I see an ad, while catching up on a gaming news site, that Angeles Comic Con is coming to Los Angeles.

It reminds me that Kasumi, who knows about everything cool before anyone else and thinks of things that we should be doing or start doing, had mentioned Angeles Comic Con. She was bummed that she'd be in Japan when it happened and emailed to say we should try going to a comic book convention sometime in the coming year. I agreed.

I've never been to a convention before. Not that I haven't wanted to go. I like nerdy things. It just hasn't been a thing I've done yet. Angeles Comic Con is not a big con. It's medium size. Just enough celebrity guests but not the biggest ones. Not the hottest exclusives but cool ones. It's not like the legendary San Diego Comic Con, which is on every nerd's bucket list, but it is local and something excellent to do this summer.

Kasumi's not here, but *I* could go. I could check it out. Do a kind of scouting mission for us. I scroll through the guests and events. It's every kind of thing that I am into. But I still hesitate because I don't know if I want to do something like that alone. It seems like something that wants to be shared. But my scrolling stops and my mind is made up when I land on their big news announcement of the day. They are going to have a panel with the cast of the upcoming Team Tomorrow film!

That settles it. How could I sit here in my Gargantua mask and not go?

This Angeles Comic Con is something I want to do.

Team Tomorrow. My favorite comic book ever. I lift my hand up to touch the mask I'm still wearing.

I start doing searches on Gargantua and pinning pictures to my various boards and posting them on social media. One website leads me to another to another, and I start learning all kinds of things about Gargantua and the history of Team Tomorrow that I didn't know, and I thought I knew it all.

With an icon like Gargantua and a team like Team Tomorrow, it's pretty easy to fall into a wormhole of information. I get lost for hours. The more I learn the deeper I go.

She's a true antihero.

I may be self-rescuing, but it's always nice to have Gargantua in your corner.

Gargantua is here to save me.

TEAM TOMORROW

Team Tomorrow has been around since 1952. It was created by Jeanne Bernier and Hal Ritko, a husband and wife team. They met overseas during the Korean War. Jeanne was a Franco-Canadian nurse and Hal worked on the newspaper doing war cartoons. They married and moved to New York, where Hal got a job drawing comics for World Comics (WC). They created a bunch of comics, but Team Tomorrow was their legacy.

A classic team favorite is Gargantua. She started off as a flagship member of Team Tomorrow, and it's said that she was modeled after Jeanne. But when Jeanne and Hal's marriage hit bottom after ten years, they divorced, and Gargantua left the core good guys team and became the head of an evil organization. Her minions, all disposable C-list villains, took to calling her *my liege*.

This was probably a rib to Jeanne by Hal, as he was widely quoted as saying that Jeanne was like a tyrant that he had to worship. Of course, due to the fact that Hal still worked at WC and because he was a man, he owned the characters. Jeanne moved back to Canada and sued him over and over again for the rights to the characters. She never won.

Hal went around calling Jeanne "that French witch" and a bunch of other horrible things. But in the turmoil of their disintegrating marriage and subsequent rights battle, one of the most formidable and iconic female superheroes/villains was born.

Two

Someone knocks on my door.

After a few days of silence filling the house and me giving my father the stink eye while he paced the floors and talked heatedly in his office, or the bathroom, or the backyard, trying desperately to make it all go away, it seems a weird thing to have to go down to Sunday breakfast and say good-bye.

"Edan." I hear my grandma Jackie on the other side of my bedroom door. Usually, I like to see her. She's the fun grandparent. The one who lives not too near but not too far. But right now she's just the reminder that things are not going well in this family. She arrived late last night after her shift at the hospital. Grandma Jackie is a pediatric cardiac surgeon, so she's no stranger to somber affairs.

She knocks on the door again, this time a bit louder.

"Edan," Grandma Jackie says again, but this time she opens the door. I'm going to yell at her, but then I stop myself. She is just doing what she's supposed to be doing. Keeping the family together in this crisis. And so I can't be mad at her for opening the door without permission. Isn't that what superheroes do sometimes? Bust down doors to do some saving and ass kicking?

Instead of opening the door and insisting that I come downstairs, I wish she could take her scalpel and fix the heart of this family. But that's not the way it works. You can't operate on a feeling.

"I'm up. I'm up," I say, and throw the blankets off of me.

"Are you still sleeping on your Team Tomorrow sheets?" she asks.

"Always," I say. "I'm never going to be too old for that."

The sheets I'm sleeping on are from the cartoon show, which is the thing that made me fall in love with the team in the first place. I've had them since I was small and they are my go-to sheets. I always feel better when I fall asleep on them. Like the team is going to take care of me while I dream.

"I still have your mother's original Star Wars sheets in storage," she says. "And some other things."

I think it's kind of cool that Grandma Jackie has kept my mom's Star Wars sheets. I wonder if she'd give them to me. I wonder what else she has tucked away that I might think is cool.

"I know this is hard," she says. "But you really need to be downstairs."

I swing myself out of the bed. I have to admit, it's an effort. I feel about as heavy as Gargantua must feel when she goes full mass.

My dad always looks put together, but somehow this morning he looks sharper than usual. He is wearing a very fine suit and his hair is perfectly coiffed. It's hard to look at him straight on, like he's blinding me with how crisp he looks.

My stomach drops, so I stop looking at him and turn to my mom. She is in a frilly bathrobe, which is weird, because she is the kind of person who dresses for breakfast and puts her face on, but right now her eyes are wet and red. A crumpled-up tissue is pushed against her nose. She keeps holding on to the edges of things, like she's going to fall down if she's not steadying herself. It makes me feel like this is all a lot worse than I already think it is.

I don't really know how to say good-bye. I kind of stand there at the kitchen island, buttering a bagel while I shuffle and look at my feet.

My dad is the one who breaks the ice.

"I hardly saw you this week, Edan," he says. Dad actually sounds a bit hurt.

He hardly saw me because I wanted to disappear from his view. I didn't want to look at him in his face and think bad thoughts.

"Do you have some plans for the summer?" he asks. He's trying desperately to connect with me before this separation happens. Trying to make small talk as though nothing is happening. That's what he does, that's what he's good at. Charm. Deflection. Misdirection. How did I never see it before?

He is acting guilty even though he insists the charges against him are false. Everyone is looking at me and I wish I could turn invisible. Or time-phase into the floor.

"There's a comic book convention," I reluctantly say. "They are making a movie of Team Tomorrow and the cast is going to be there."

"Your favorite," he says.

I nod. Surprised that he knows anything about me at all.

"Maybe you could send me a copy of it so I can see what you like about it," he says. "I think I'll be doing a lot of reading."

That kind of punches me in the guts. Here he is looking dapper and trying to be cheery, and Mom is pretty much crying, and I'm being surly, and really *his* whole life is about to change.

I feel like a little girl again. And for one brief second I don't care if he's the bad guy in my story. Even if he might be a thief and if the things I've overheard are true, that he did mess around with production payrolls. He is my dad, and despite how pissed off I am, I am going to miss him.

I go to him like I'm five years old and don't know anything about the world, and I throw my arms around him and bury my head in his chest, and he ruffles my hair like when I was little.

"I'll be back soon," he says.

The kitchen door opens and Bobby, one of his business partners, steps in. He looks just as dapper and they say some stuff to each other. I don't know if it's because I haven't been able to eat the bagel I made or because my heart is beating really hard, but everything is kind of in a fog now. It's muffled and it's hard to hear.

Dad turns and waves at us like he's going to get some milk or something and not up north to be put under a magnifying glass.

"Good-bye, then," he says, and then he leaves. He is gone.

Once the door closes behind him, my mom rushes straight to her room. Grandma Jackie sits herself at the kitchen table, nursing a cold cup of coffee. I hover by the closed door, like I can see through it, watching the car that is leaving, driving down the road, all the way to the uncertain future that is ours. I want to be able to see into tomorrow.

"Well, what kinds of plans do you have for today?" Grandma Jackie asks, breaking the silence, trying to keep things normal.

"I think I'm going to go back to bed," I say.

"I think you should go take a walk," she says. "It's a beautiful day."

"I don't think so," I say. "Mom went back to bed, so I think I can go into a cave, too."

Grandma Jackie stares at me for a good long moment, and then she digs into her purse and gives me a twenty-dollar bill.

"I need you to run an errand for me," she says. "Go to the Sunday farmers' market down the street and pick up some fresh flowers. This house could use some color."

I weigh the situation. I could ignore her and go to the family room, turn off all the lights, and keep playing video games. That would be a compromise of a kind. I wouldn't be going back to bed, I'd be doing something. Or I could take her money, take the walk, and use the change to buy myself a coffee. Because I know that I don't have an allowance anymore. I don't have money. And this is going to be it if I want to ever go out and get a cappuccino again.

It's not unlike when Gargantua, in the battle of the North and South (Team Tomorrow issues 52–58) punched Magnetic Pole so hard that her polarity reversed and she became unable to navigate, going down when she wanted to go up. Going east when she wanted to go west. It wreaked havoc on all of her teammates during a few fights and she had to be grounded. It's one of the reasons Gargantua had to leave. After her family was wiped out of time, she couldn't find north. No one could.

I accept the money without saying a word and pad up to my room to put my clothes on.

There is always time to play games and become darker. A little time in the sun won't change that.

It didn't change Gargantua. She still went dark no matter how much Green Guarder tried to bring her into the sun.

Three

eing outside doesn't make me feel any better. Standing in the middle of the flower tent surrounded by color and smell doesn't make me feel better. Drinking a double doesn't make me feel better.

The only thing that saves the day is a text from Kasumi asking me for a Skype chat.

Do you know how good it feels to see your best friend's face when you are feeling low? *So good.* My heart is lifted by her voice. Her head looks small on my screen, but she is a sight for sore eyes.

"How is Japan?" I ask, sitting at one of the temporary pop-up table tents at the market.

"Oh, it's the best," she says. "I blew my manga and anime budget in two days. And I've taken a ton of great pictures."

Kasumi is a great photographer. She is in Japan because her dad, a cinematographer, is shooting a movie there and took the whole family for summer vacation. After our initial hellos and blowing kisses and her telling me all about Japan (I want to go there one day) and the movie and the crush she has on one of the girls in the crew, she asks about me.

"Wait, why are you wearing that mask?" she asks.

"I'm trying to pull together a Gargantua costume for Angeles Comic Con," I say. I'd forgotten that I was wearing it.

"Oh my gosh, jealous!" she says. "We should be going to that together."

"I figured I'd check it out for us," I say.

"So you're going to cosplay?" she asks. "I'd like to cosplay. I'd maybe be Katana or Gamora or Wonder Woman."

"You'd look great as all of those," I say.

"Wait," she says. "I thought you were going to be out of town for it when I mentioned it to you?"

"I'm not now," I say. "Stuff happened."

"What?" she asks. I shake my head. I watch as a cat walks across the desk in front of her. And then I realize that I don't want to say it.

"It's nothing," I say.

She opens her eyes wide and makes a face. She knows me too well. You can't hide anything from your best friend, especially when you've known each other since fourth grade. She knows everything about my face and all of my tells. Not even this mask can cover up the way I purse my mouth.

"Stuff," I say. "My dad had to go away. So the summer is kind of messed up."

"What's up?" she asks. "Are they separating or something?"

"Something like that," I say. Which in Kasumi's mind means yes. I don't correct her, because my parents separating is way more understandable than my dad being sequestered because the entertainment payroll company he works for may or may not have done something shady and there might be a trial. I don't tell her that I feel a dread in the pit of my stomach that I can't get rid of.

"Oh, man, Edan, I'm so sorry," she says.

I am glad I am wearing the mask so that she can't see I'm about to cry.

"It totally sucks. My mom is a wreck. My grandma Jackie is here taking care of us."

Kasumi puts her arms out to hug the camera.

"Virtual hug," she says. "Virtual hugs."

I lift my arms up to hug her back. Somehow, even though her arms are thousands of miles away, the very act of the virtual hug does make me feel better.

"So instead I'm going to be doing stuff around here," I say. "It's all right."

I make it sound like I'm really busy, even though everyone seems to be mostly away for the summer doing something. The people who are in town, like Yuri Ross, who I have a crush on, and the Ferrar twins, Joss and Gwen, have asked me to do stuff, but I can't afford to do the things they want to do, so I just keep brushing them off to the point where I'm sure they've pretty much given up on me.

"Well, you know who's a big nerd? Yuri! You should ask to go to Angeles Comic Con with him," Kasumi says.

I look at her like I'm pretend shocked that she knows who my biggest crush is. I have been crushing on him from afar all sophomore year. I call him "the glancer" because even though we barely speak to each other, he glances at me a lot in class.

"I don't know that I can just ask him," I say. "We don't know him that well."

"Sure you can!" Kasumi says. She's one million times braver than I am. "He posted online that he was going. His mom is on a panel or something. He has a spare badge that he's been trying to get rid of for weeks."

"Oh, yeah," I say. I remember seeing that.

"I'm so glad I don't like boys," Kasumi says.

Then Kasumi and I troubleshoot a bunch of ways that I could approach Yuri and still seem cool and not desperate. We settle on me sending a casual text the day of the convention. Like, *Hey there, I'm here.*

"I'm most excited because there is going to be a Team Tomorrow panel, with the director and cast."

"Get out!" Kasumi says. And even though she really only likes the cartoon and never really crossed over to reading the comic books, she starts doing a little dance in front of the screen. That's what friends do. They comfort you. They know you. And I wish I weren't lying and that Kasumi were here and not thousands of miles away and in a different time zone so that we could have a sleepover and I could tell her the truth.

I want to pretend for just a little longer that everything is exactly the same as it is supposed to be.

That my life is right side up and not upside down.

TEAM TOMORROW

For a while, Team Tomorrow had slipped from an A comic to a C comic. It was mostly forgotten in the mid-sixties. It had a core audience that continued to read it regularly, but it was not as popular as DC or Marvel titles. But in the late 1980s, it was acquired and optioned and made into a morning cartoon. The cartoon lasted two seasons but was notable for having in its animation pedigree some of the most important creators in their first jobs.

Nearly every animator who worked on the show went on to create some of the most beloved cartoons on the air today. Because of this, and the general high quality of the animation and before-its-time risks the show took, it became available on streaming services. The emotional wit, clever puns, and brilliant drawing brought Team Tomorrow to a whole new generation. One that was ready for it.

This cemented the resurgence of the team, which had never gone away but had not yet come into its own.

Four

A week after my dad is sequestered, I ride-share over to the convention center, wearing my makeshift Gargantua costume. I look pretty decent for someone who pulled the costume together from my closet in just a few days. They call that closet cosplay. Still, it's nothing compared to some of the costumes I see when I exit the car.

I thank the driver and then tug on my costume, as though somehow that will magically make it better. I know I could probably up my game next time. If there is a next time.

"My liege." A lady wearing a Team Tomorrow shirt flourishes a bow to me. She addresses me as though I really am Gargantua, saluting me like one of her henchmen, and that makes me feel like I'm really ten feet tall.

I smile. My first in days.

This is good, I think.

When I get there, I text Yuri, in my opinion the cutest boy *ever*. I have had the text ready since I talked with Kasumi. We crafted it to be casual and forward.

Hey. It's Edan Kupferman. I'm outside at Angeles Comic Con. Any chance you still have that extra badge?

While I wait for him to text me back, I sit on a tree planter and take in the scene.

There is a steady stream of nerds (my people) and cosplayers filing into the convention center. Even those who aren't cosplaying their favorite character pretty much have some kind of nerdy T-shirt or dress on. There is not one kind of geekery that is not represented. There are comic book geeks. Sci-fi geeks. Fantasy geeks. Science geeks. Vampire geeks. Goth geeks. Time travel geeks. History geeks. Horror geeks. Tabletop gamer geeks. RPG geeks. Video game geeks. Space enthusiast geeks. *Every. Kind. Of. Geek.*

A few more people pass me by and give me the little Team Tomorrow *my liege* bow with a flourish.

Gargantua is ten feet tall. And people have to look up to her. In my life, people usually look down to me because I am only four feet ten. It's a relief to be here, as her, and to be bowed to since I don't want to be myself. It's as though I feel myself growing in her skin.

My phone pings. It's a message from Yuri.

Edan! Ahhhhhh! Someone else snagged it. I would have totally given it to you.

"Crap," I say to no one in particular.

Cool, I type back. *I'll figure it out.*

Try to buy one. Text me when you get in. :D

I head up to the ticket kiosk and wait in line. And I'm looking at the prices. Seventy-five dollars for the weekend. Twenty-five dollars for the day.

I step up to the window and take out my dad's emergency credit card.

"One weekend badge," I say.

"Sorry, honey," the woman in the yellow volunteer T-shirt says. "We're all sold out."

"What about for today only?" I ask.

She shakes her head.

"Then what is this line for?" I ask.

"People who are having trouble accessing their bar code," she says. "Mostly I get asked where the bathrooms are."

I whip off my mask to press my eyes to stop tears from flowing. I'm so close to my goal and so far away. To make things worse, it seems like things could go really well with Yuri if I could just get inside the convention.

"You're going to have to move along," the woman says. "You're holding up the line."

"Hey, don't I go to school with you?" I hear an unfamiliar voice ask as I step off to the side of the line.

I look up and shade my eyes. It's a guy around my age who I don't recognize. His hair is dark and a little too long, like Han Solo at any age, or hero-in-a-1970/80s-movie longish. His eyes are so dark that you can't tell where the brown begins and the cornea starts. He is wearing a Team Tomorrow T-shirt I've never seen before, and it is so worn out and full of holes that it must be original vintage.

I want it.

"Marshall High?" I ask.

He nods. I nod.

"I guess so," I say.

"I was in your history class. Mr. Martinez. I came in half-way through the year," he said.

I look at him again.

"I needed a change," he says as though that explains it.

Then I shrug. I don't care about when he came to school. I've got a bucketful of troubles of my own.

"You going in?" he asks, flipping his thumb at the convention center.

"I don't have a badge," I say. "I thought I had a hookup, but I don't. And it's sold out."

"Has been for months. It's a hot ticket."

"Perfect. My summer is turning out just perfect."

"You really have to plan for these things," he says. "Comic Cons are very popular."

"Well, I am figuring that out. And now that I have, my day is ruined," I complain. I blink a few times, because when I say my day is ruined, I mean I feel as though my life is ruined. "So I'm just going to leave and go back to my evil lair."

He laughs and then cocks his head to the side and looks at me.

"Gargantua wouldn't be bummed about it," he says after a moment of sizing me up. "She'd just storm the place."

"Yeah," I say. "My powers are kind of depleted right now."

He looks at me again, and this time when he does, it's like he's using some kind of X-ray vision to look right inside of me. Like he sees that I'm sad. That something is wrong. That I could use a break.

"It's your lucky day," he says. "My mom bailed on me today so I've got an extra badge."

"Seriously?" I ask.

"Yeah," he says. Then he pulls out two badges from his man bag, puts one on himself, and offers the other one to me. "You are now Flora Gomez."

"I can't pay you back," I say.

"Come on, *my liege*," he says as he cocks his head to motion for me to follow him to the convention center.

Part of me is like *No way*. I'm not going into a convention center with a boy I might have been in a class with who is definitely a stranger. Then the other part of me is like *Whatever*. Gargantua never said no to an adventure. And besides, the more I look at him, the more he does look familiar. And besides, he's helping me out just when I need a miracle. Team Tomorrow always says that help for today might have come from yesterday. This feels like one of those kind of moments.

Then he sticks out his hand. "Hi, I'm Kirk Gomez."

"Hi, I'm Edan Kupferman," I say.

"Edan," he says. "That's right. I remember now."

"Thanks," I say, shaking my badge, which is now around my neck. "You really saved the day."

"No problem," he says.

When we get inside to the lobby of the very crowded convention center, I wonder if I'm going to be obliged to hang out with him, but before I can make some excuse like I have to go to the bathroom so I can ditch him, he looks at me sheepishly.

"So I gotta go 'cause there is something I have to do, and then there's a panel I want to see that I want to get a seat for. So if it's cool, I'm going to ditch you."

"Yeah," I say, relieved at his candor. "It's cool."

"Cool," he says. "Have a good time at the show, Edan. See you at school."

"Yeah," I say.

Then he pivots and sprints up the escalator and I am free to wander the convention on my own.

I glance around the lobby, and I'm overwhelmed. It really is like I've stepped through a door. Like I'm in Oz. Or Wonderland. Or another planet. There are colors and flashing lights and sounds. There are costumes galore. There are people with bags full to the brim with toys and books and stuff. The exhibition floor is packed and the dealer tables are filled with a million things that I want to buy. Cute nerdy girl T-shirts. Adorable action figures. Must-have plushies. Rad posters. Original fan art. Ephemera of all sorts. Geek chic clothing.

Maybe putting together this Gargantua costume channeled her luck for me a little bit.

Gargantua is magical like that. Always willing people to do what she wants. Always getting what she needs just when you think it is all over for her. Always growing ten feet tall when she needs to.

I put my mask back on and immediately feel better about everything.

five

I go from booth to booth to booth, fingering all the things I want, taking business cards from the dealers so I can later order online some of the amazing but really expensive stuff I am finding. I imagine how great I'll look at school in all of the Team Tomorrow dresses I would get. But it's not just Team Tomorrow that has me smitten. It's *everything*. It's like I've cracked open a part of myself that has been there all along. I rediscover fandoms I am already a fan of.

I've been a nerd my whole life, but never embraced it fully. It never crossed my mind to pursue it, so I've never been to a con before. And now that I'm at one, I don't know how I will ever stop going to them.

These are my people.

Knowing that makes me feel slightly better, no matter how much fun I'm missing by not being on a trip near a body of water somewhere or not being able to fully hang out with my friends here in the city. If I had done either of those, I'd be missing out on this. This magical wonderful thing. This thing that Kasumi and I should have been coming to for years.

Everyone I talk to says this a medium-size convention, but the place feels enormous and there is a seemingly endless number of things to see and do.

I love that I get all the little inside jokes and T-shirt quotes. *Chewie Is My Copilot. Keep Calm and Call Kamala Khan. Team Bella Dumps Them Both and Goes to College. My Other Car Is a TARDIS.*

But my favorite, my absolute favorite, is from Team Tomorrow. *Tomorrow Is only Yesterday to Today.*

I have to buy it.

I take out the emergency credit card and give it to the pink-haired, tattooed girl at the booth. She swipes it and it is declined.

"Declined, sweetie," she says. "Got another, or better yet, cash?"

I don't have another and I don't have any cash. Then it hits me. Of course my dad's emergency credit card isn't going to work. Nothing is going to work. There is no emergency backup.

I can't buy a single thing here.

The thing is, when your dad's being sequestered, you don't really get an allowance anymore. I have been very used to having an allowance or just asking him for money, and now I pretty much have only enough to buy lunch and ride-share back home.

I turn bright red and quickly put the T-shirt back down on the table. I have to let it go.

"Can I take your business card? I'll just order it online," I say.

She sweetly hands me a card and then looks at me.

"Hang on," she says. She opens up her cashbox and hands me another card. "Enter that secret code when you do and you'll get a 15 percent discount and free shipping in California."

"Thanks," I say. It is such a genuinely nice thing to do. I can tell that she doesn't do it for everyone.

"Anything for you, my liege." She smiles as she does the hand flourish.

I tug at my Gargantua costume. It's certainly been my good-luck charm in my growing bad situation.

I check my phone and realize that it's almost time to go up to catch the *Team Tomorrow* panel.

I weave my way through the thickening crowd and head to the main hall and up the escalator to where the panels are taking place. And gasp! There is a line that goes all the way around and back again several times.

"Is this for *Team Tomorrow*?" I ask no one in particular.

"Good luck getting in," I'm told by someone dressed as Rey from *Star Wars: The Force Awakens* who is walking away from the line. "I'm going to go to a different panel."

I stare at the line. It is very long. It wraps and wraps and curves and goes all the way down the hall. I can't even see the end of it. I'm surprised and then I'm not. I always thought that Team Tomorrow was my own private thing. That somehow it was this obscure fandom that no one else liked like I did. But of course it's not. It's huge. And today is the first day that the whole cast is going to be together talking about the film. It shouldn't surprise me that the panel is going to be crazy packed.

But, still, the size of the crowd leaves me gobsmacked.

"Edan!" I hear my name being called. "There you are!"

I turn, and in the thick of the line, at a place that is sure to get in, I see Yuri and his friends Phil and Tze.

"I told you the bathroom line would be long, girl," Yuri says and then waves to me to come over and join them.

I look behind me and then to the people in the line.

"Excuse me," I say. "I gotta get to my boyfriend."

I smile a little as I say *boyfriend*, because it's a wish, not the truth.

"Tough. No cuts," says a weird alien from a film or TV show I don't recognize.

"Edan!" Yuri says. He points at me. *She's with me*, he mouths to the weird alien.

"Coming," I say.

The alien doesn't budge and then raises a hand to block me.

"Look, it's my time of the month and this costume took forever to undo. Cut me a break, won't you?" I say.

"Come on," a lady dressed as Tri Star, Team Tomorrow's newest team member, says to the alien. "It's one person."

Tristar pulls my arm so I can make it through the line.

"Thanks," I say.

"No problem, my liege," Tri Star says.

I hurry my way over to Yuri and he immediately puts his arm around my waist.

"Hey, honey," he says, making a big show to the weird alien, like I really am his girlfriend. "You made it."

"Thanks," I say. "I really wanted to see this panel."

"I didn't know you were such a big Team Tomorrow fan," Yuri says. "That's so unexpectedly cool."

"I am a big fan," I say. "I like lots of things, but they are the best."

"What did Eldorado say to Gargantua on Planet Genghis?" Phil cuts in on my moment with Yuri.

"What?" I ask.

"So you don't know?" Phil says with a smirk.

Yuri gives me a look to go with it, or maybe it's a look that is him waiting for the answer, too, I can't tell. So I just go with it because they are his friends and he got me this place in line ensuring that I would get into the panel.

"No, I do know. Gargantua said, 'The thought of tomorrow is what we see today,'" I say. "But why would you ask me that?"

"How many different outfits has Gargantua had?" Tze asks.

I start to protest again, but Yuri's hand sort of touches my arm, kind of calming me, kind of saying that he thinks his friends are being dumb, too. So I let go of the flare of anger that could make me go Gargantua full size and just start thinking, *Oh my gosh, Yuri is touching me.*

I want to kick myself a little bit, because I am fully aware that I am being swayed by the touch of a cute boy. That's not how I was raised or how I feel, but now that I'm in the moment, with Yuri touching me, I kind of can't help myself. I feel a little bit soft inside. I wonder if that's why Gargantua had to get away from Green Guarder. He made her feel less sure of herself? Less large. I feel both vulnerable and large. It's very dizzying. So instead of saying, *No, I'm not going to answer these stupid questions*, I open my mouth and answer.

"Five," I say before I do a proper count in my head.

Yuri starts to say something, but I interrupt him, holding up my hand to shush him. "Unless you count her clones, then seven."

We both smile.

"Who is Freego?" Tze asks.

"Green Guarder's time-lost son," I say. "Why are you asking me these things?"

I've had enough of the quizzing.

"Just checking," Phil says.

"Come on, guys," Yuri says. Then he touches my arm again and turns to face me with his cute-as-all-get-out face. "I guess you *are* a real fan."

"Of course I'm a real fan," I say. "I'm standing here at a comic book convention wearing a freaking Gargantua costume!"

"You could be faking it," Tze says, shrugging like it's still unclear if I'm a real fan or not.

I let it slide, because I don't know what exactly they are getting at, especially as they are dressed in jeans and T-shirts (not even Team Tomorrow T-shirts!) and I am standing in front of them wearing purple spandex tights with silver stitching and a black G painted across my chest and a mask.

"Hardly," I say. "Besides, I imagine that everyone standing here in this ridiculously long line at Angeles Comic Con is a *real* fan."

"Maybe not her," Yuri says, pointing to a girl wearing a very revealing costume. "She's probably not really a fan."

Honestly, I can't tell what she's supposed to be. A sexy fairy? A maybe medieval lady? An elf?

"Well, she's a fan of something," I say. "Maybe that's her D&D character or someone from a YA book that we haven't read. They are all real fans."

"I'm a fan of all the skin I'm seeing right now," Tze says.

"Oh my gosh, Tze," I say. "Quit it."

"Ha, ha, ha," he says.

The boys punch each other on the shoulders. I crinkle my brow, wondering if I should say something more in defense of the girl, of all girls, really.

"Don't listen to them," Yuri says to me, his fingers squeezing me just a little, and I flutter. "They've just never seen this many ladies looking that good all at once."

"There are good-looking girls at school," I say as they open the door and the line starts to shift.

"Fair point," Phil says.

"But it's fantasy central here," Tze says. "Doesn't compare."

"Well, just don't be a jerk about it," I say, finally finding a little bit of my voice again. "These girls are having their fan fun just like you are."

They all laugh with me. Or maybe it's actually at me. I can't really tell. But I put the thought away for the moment because the line starts to move and everyone is focused on getting in the room and getting seats. Yuri's arm is still around me, and it makes me feel pretty good. I wonder if he knows that he's still touching me. I am hyperaware of it.

He only lets go of me when we are settled in our seats. Then, Yuri and his friends start quizzing one another on Team Tomorrow, trying to one-up one another, and I guess that's the way it goes. It makes me feel a bit better about the quizzing they did to me, and I even jump in every once in a while when one of them gets stumped, and it's pretty fun. The weird moment that I felt before passes.

I feel like I'm one of the group.

Like I found my team.

Six

Keisha Johnson, the director of *Team Tomorrow*, takes the stage and the whole room bursts into applause, except the boys surrounding me.

"Just look how cool she is," I say. She's standing on the side of the podium, laughing with the guy who is probably the film executive. He's kind of a thin, nervous white guy. She is a beautiful black woman. Her hair is piled up in a bunch of braids on top of her head. She's wearing big, chunky jewelry and the Team Tomorrow shirt that I wanted, only hers is bedazzled.

As though she wasn't already, she's immediately my hero.

"Fashion goals," I say.

"She does look hot. But the real test is whether or not the movie holds up, don't you think?" Yuri says.

Of course he has a point. Still, I ignore him.

"It must be so cool to flesh out characters that people love so much and bring them to the screen," I say.

Keisha Johnson started with an indie film that won the audience award at Sundance. After that, she was given the reins for a larger studio picture, an all-female reboot of the 1980s film *Sneakers*. That's when her career took off and she did an action war thriller and then a huge ghost story and now she's finally doing her first comic book movie.

"I just hope she doesn't mess it up," Phil leans over and says to the others. "I don't know why they got her to direct this movie."

I know I heard Phil say it, but I can't believe I heard it. It's like a bucket of ice was thrown on me. I freeze even more when Tze and Yuri groan in agreement.

I'm trying in my mind to figure out what they are so worried about. Keisha Johnson's known for big-budget action movies. She's a professional with box office megahits under her belt. Every interview I've read since my bingeing on everything Team Tomorrow assures me that she knows the characters and the team well and has a vision. Personally, I'm not worried. I know that she's going to do an amazing job. I just feel it in my bones.

"As long as things blow up and the action scenes are cool, then it's all good," Yuri says. I notice Yuri kind of glancing at me and checking my face, which I am trying to hold in a neutral position as I try to sort out the sexism I'm hearing happening around me. I realize it's not just Phil. As I listen, I hear other groups around me saying the same kinds of things.

What is wrong with them?

Yuri can tell that I'm going to lose it and he's trying to calm me down. He puts his arm around my shoulder and pulls me in.

"Of course she's going to blow things up, and of course it's going to be good," I say to him. I hate that I sound like I'm pouting, but sometimes it seems like sincere insistence comes off sounding false.

"Well, you never know," Yuri says. "I mean, there are plenty of comic book movies that just kind of suck."

His saying that makes me feel both better and worse. He's not wrong. There are plenty of films that seem like they are going to be good and then are terrible. You watch the trailer and you are blown away, and *pfffffft*, you go opening weekend, and fifteen minutes in, it is a major yawn.

I glance over at Keisha Johnson and the moderator, who are taking photographs. A man who looks like a studio publicist is coordinating the whole thing and he keeps looking at his phone, to keep things on schedule. There are a few more minutes before the panel officially starts; you can feel the fan buzz in the room, which is so crowded that the volunteers are asking people to raise their hands if they have an empty seat next to them, as there are people looking for seats and even waiting to get into the room.

I sit quietly as Yuri and Phil and Tze start talking about all the comic book movies that they hate and how they were ruined, and they start listing all of these film directors who totally messed them up and how these other filmmakers would have done better. Even though some of the filmmakers they recommend are people who messed up some of the movies they are talking about. It's like a circular illogical argument where everyone is right and if you disagree, then you are stupid.

I keep my mouth shut, and a part of me leans away from them because with Phil leading the way, they are being embarrassing and I'm afraid people around me might think I agree with them.

I'm about to reach my boiling point and say something, but then the audience bursts into applause as Keisha Johnson walks to the podium and the panel formally starts.

Keisha Johnson starts talking about the comic book and how it influenced her growing up.

"There is a rich history with Team Tomorrow. Jeanne Bernier was a pioneer in comics. The fact that she was suppressed by her husband and had to fight her whole life for co-ownership of the characters she created is a fascinating story in and of itself."

She talks about representation, citing the character Magnetic Pole as a personal hero.

"I saw myself in Magnetic Pole, a young, strong black woman who had the power to change where north pointed. That was what I aspired to do with my career."

She talks about writing the script and how many different versions they had before they settled on the story they wanted to tell.

When superhero movies are made, they usually go for the broadest, easiest-to-follow story.

Studios must consider many factors to make a successful transition from page to screen. Which team lineup was the movie going to have? Which universe would it be set in?

Original? Pre-Schism? Schism II? Reborn? New Galaxy? Starting Point?

The WC had rebooted Team Tomorrow a million times.

You could ask many different fans which their favorite incarnation of Team Tomorrow was, and you would get a different answer every time.

The hardest thing for any studio is to minimize spoilers while doling out enough information about a film to hook the fans.

Everything about the Team Tomorrow film must be shrouded in secrecy.

"There are so many ways that we could have gone with Team Tomorrow, so many favorite story arcs. We can't do everything in a two-hour film, but I think you'll like where we start."

"Blah, blah, blah," Phil mutters.

"Shh," I say. I want to hear more. I've been deep-diving into Team Tomorrow, reading all about its creators and the team history. You can really fall into a wormhole once you start, and every new tidbit I get is like a new piece of golden information about the hearts of the characters I love.

"Do you want to meet the team?" Keisha Johnson asks the audience.

We all scream.

"Do you want to see what tomorrow looks like?" she asks the audience.

We are whipped up into a frenzy.

Keisha Johnson waves her hands to quiet us down.

"Let me introduce you," she says, "to your Team Tomorrow!"

The actors come on stage as she calls them up one by one. I am amongst the first people to get up on my feet. I am clapping and hooting and whistling and screaming.

Green Guarder! Tri Star! Magnetic Pole! Gargantua! Lady Bird! Split Second!

When the woman playing Gargantua comes out, for a moment I gasp. Of course I'd seen pictures on the web, but when I see her in person, just wearing civilian clothes, I know she's perfect. Tall, muscular, not too beautiful, not too plain. She is absolutely perfect.

The actors wave and smile as they take their seats.

I immediately wonder why certain characters aren't there. I wonder if they are keeping any characters secret. I wonder what story they are going to tell. I have my ideas based on who is on the stage, but you can never tell. They swap out story lines all the time in comic book movies, giving plot elements to a different character. Sometimes it works. Sometimes it doesn't.

The host from Nerdist, wearing an amazing Lady Bird–inspired dress, leads a panel discussion with the team. The actors are charming and fun and laughing and they know the characters really well. They start a slide show that clicks along and shows a bunch of concept art slides, and the actors answer questions about their characters coyly. They can't say anything and they don't want to spoil anything.

"All I can tell you, it's going to be fun, right, Gargantua?" the actor playing Green Guarder says, looking coyly at the actress playing Gargantua at the other side of the podium.

The way they are joking and flirting, it seems as though they are going to restart the love story between Green Guarder and Gargantua, which is one of my least favorite runs of Team Tomorrow.

I like it when she becomes the villain. When she gets her minions. When she tries to fix the time rip of tomorrow on her own. When she gets the world to call her *my liege*.

"What?" I say. "Barf. Did they just hint at a love story? Between good and evil?"

I always felt that Gargantua and Green Guarder weren't a perfect match. He's too good. She's too complex. It could never really work. I liked it better when Gargantua went full evil and had an affair with Split Second. Split Second, pure evil, always bringing them back to their first kiss in a loop.

Green Guarder just loved and loved and loved her. Through all of time. Once, he even went back all the way to the first moment and punched the universe so it would go one way and not another just to spare her more pain and misery. He loved her that much. I don't know that I believe in that kind of grand gesture.

"Eh, who cares about the romance part?" Yuri says. "Look at the mecha robot the bad guys have!"

Yuri points to a slide where Gargantua is in the middle of a pile of rubble on a city street with an army of mecha robots.

She's got her capelet blowing in the wind, her G is shining like a bright beacon on her mask, and she's tall as hell.

She looks like she's just seized the world.

I'm looking in awe at the pictures as they click by.

It's pretty amazing. It's them. It's really them. It's Team Tomorrow.

Suddenly everything is a little bit better.

"I think there is no doubt that it's going to be good," I say to Yuri excitedly, and I squeeze his arm.

"Yeah," Yuri says. "Looks good."

"Probably," Phil says. "But you never know."

"Always room to blow it," Tze says.

How can they be excited and cynical at the same time? Is it their version of playing it cool? It seems so tiring to try to be like that, wary of everything. I am wary of everything lately and it exhausts me.

The unsaid thing that Phil and Tze leave hanging in the air, the undercurrent, and it deflates me, is that the film is being directed by a woman. But I shake that off. I'm not going to be disappointed and that is paramount.

"Oh and before I forget," Keisha Johnson adds, "we'll be holding a cosplay contest at San Diego Comic Con, where we'll be premiering the film. The winner with the best Team Tomorrow outfit will get to be an extra on the set of the sequel. And yes, that means we've already been green-lit for a sequel."

The crowd cheers.

"We'll fly you out to the set and you'll have three days rolling with the cast and crew. You'll get to experience a little bit of what it's like being on the team."

The cast and director say good-bye and exit the stage, waving. I jump to my feet and I am wolf whistling and screaming and clapping my hands so hard that they smart. If the audience went crazy before, it was nothing. The place is going absolutely wild.

Even after they are long gone, I am still standing and hollering with joy.

"I am going to win that contest," I say.

"Not with that outfit, you're not," Yuri says.

Yuri's not being mean. He's telling the truth. I look around the room. I can spot about a dozen Gargantuas and they all look better than me. My costume is not up to snuff. I'm going to have to get serious about my cosplay if I'm going to stand any chance of winning.

I didn't know how I was going to fill my days this summer.

And now I know.

I'm going to learn how to make a costume so great that it pulls me right out of my misery and changes my life.

Seven

"How was it?" Kasumi asks over Skype.

"It was great. Yuri got me in," I say. I mean to the panel, but she cuts me off before I can specify.

"Right," Kasumi says. "You and Yuri. I love it. Did he ask you out?"

"The line was crazy long, and Yuri pretended that he was my boyfriend so I could cut in line . . ."

"Ahhh!" Kasumi says. "He loooooooooves you."

"No," I say. "I mean, he said, *See you around*. But I don't know what that means."

"That's kind of like an invitation to hang out," she says. "You should ask him out, now that you're going to be in town all summer."

"I guess so," I say. "I'll put it on my to-do list."

"To-do list! Doesn't he have a pool at his house? Doesn't he live in, like, a mansion?"

"I don't think it's a mansion, I think it's just nice," I say. "His dad is an agent. His mom writes for TV."

"Exactly," Kasumi says. "Put on a bikini, bike over to his mansion, and make him your man."

I laugh out loud.

I tell her about the cosplay contest for Team Tomorrow and her eyes light up.

"You have to win," she says.

"I know," I say. "But my cosplay skills aren't the best."

"We can work on this," she says. Kasumi is always so optimistic about things. She's never seen a challenge that she can't meet head-on. It's what I admire and love about her. And probably why we've been such close friends since the fourth grade. We can keep up with each other like no one else can. I don't know what I'd do without her. I don't how I'm getting through this summer without her.

"This is a skill that can be learned. That's what YouTube is for!" she says.

"School just sent out the club petition form," I say. "I was thinking of starting a cosplay club at school."

"You don't need a club to make a costume."

"I know," I say. "It'd just be more fun. More social."

I'm so antisocial right now that I feel like having a club is just the thing to force me to focus my energies and connect with something. It's like I'm turtling in my house. Or I've retreated to my secret lair. I need a reason to come out eventually.

"Oh! That *is* a perfect idea," Kasumi says. "Besides, running a club looks good on a college application. It shows character."

I breathe a sigh of relief. I've been so insecure because of my life in turmoil that I've been worried that everything I think of doing is dumb.

"But we need at least ten people to gain club status and have access to a room," I say.

"Make a group online and I'll help you recruit people from here in Japan. We've got six weeks. And me plus you already makes two. Only eight to go."

"Maybe I could ask Yuri and the boys," I say. "They're always going to cons."

"That's a great idea. What about the Ferrar twins? They're nerds, they'll join," Kasumi says.

"Yes, totally," I say. And I think it is a good way to touch base with Joss and Gwen since I've been blowing off their emails and texts the past few weeks.

There is a break in the conversation. And I take a deep breath and decide that I'm going to confess about what's going on in my home life.

"Kasumi, there's something I was going to tell you . . ."

"Hold that thought," she says. She then turns her head and I hear someone offscreen, talking in Japanese. "I'm sorry, Edan. I gotta go. Family time."

Time zones suck.

"OK," I say. "I'll catch you later."

She blows me a kiss and I blow her one back.

"You're ridiculous and I love you," she says. She makes a

kissy-face and leans into the camera. She's laughing and I'm laughing, and I miss laughing so much.

"Gosh, it was good to see your face," I say.

"You, too," Kasumi says.

The screen goes blank. I'm left hanging a little bit. I wanted to tell her what was going on. Like I've been super thwacked, kapow into the air.

But now I've got a plan to get me through summer. A goal for when I can stitch my life back together.

Learn to sew. Date Yuri. Become Gargantua.

Things are always better when you've got a plan.

I'm going to assemble my own team. There will be Superheroes Everywhere.

TEAM TOMORROW

When the first issue of Team Tomorrow came out in 1954, the team was small. There were only four characters:

Gargantua had height and strength and genius-level intelligence.

Green Guarder had the ability to make plants and people bloom around him. His strength was gained from the sun.

Figment's ability was to revise memory.

Magnetic Pole had full control of polarity and direction.

The characters were of their time. They were a reaction to the politics of the day. They were also a fractured mirror of the struggles between a husband and wife. You can see clearly Jeanne's struggle to be a modern woman in a world that was still not ready to accept equality for women. In an era when gender roles were very black and white, there wasn't room for women with a sense of independence and power. Jeanne fought against that with her master character, Gargantua. A woman who literally towered over men in order to be heard.

It is no wonder that women of the age coined terms like "I'm going Gargantua" as a code to one another about being heard in spaces where traditionally a woman was voiceless.

When a woman invoked this, men smiled, but understanding the reference, they subliminally took a moment to listen. This is why Gargantua is a feminist icon. Giving voice in a time when women were made to consistently feel small.

It's a legacy that still serves today, in an America where women, while having made strides over the past seventy years, still are marginalized and butt up against a glass ceiling.

Eight

It takes exactly one week of texting and commenting on social media to get Yuri to clue in and ask me to come over and play video games with him.

When I get ready, I'm really excited. I think about how it's going to be just the two of us hanging out. I wonder if I can call it a date? I call it a date in my head. Like, it's a date! Even though it's just a hang.

I imagine how the day will go. I'll impress him with my gaming skills and then we'll maybe hold hands or something more. Me and Yuri Ross making out! I try to visualize it and I get goose bumps.

I change my outfit a bunch of times, making a mess of clothes on the bathroom floor that Grandma Jackie tells me to "pick up." To which I reply, "Later."

Grandma Jackie is the team captain of this house now. She watches my mom like a hawk. Putting food and liquids in front of her. Clucking at her to eat. Picking up the things that my mother trails behind her. Robe. Towels. Shoes.

It's not unlike when Gargantua watched over Green Guarder when he temporarily lost his abilities in their fight with the enemy Solar Flare. Green Guarder took power from the sun, but like for a plant, it had to be the right amount. Too much sun weakened him. He turned pale and translucent. He crisped at his edges. Green Guarder didn't like being helpless and dependent on her, and Gargantua resented being needed. When he got well, Green Guarder thanked Gargantua by making a special oversize garden for her where she could feel normal size when she got all big. He was just doing what he knew how to do. Make things bloom.

But Gargantua couldn't handle it. She bickered the whole time she was helping him. Never mind that it also made the team miserable. And then when she left, a heartbroken Green Guarder let the garden die.

My mother bickers with my grandmother, and I bicker with them both. And no one has watered our garden this summer at all.

Most of the time these days, it's just Grandma Jackie and me at the kitchen table for breakfast, lunch, and dinner. Mom doesn't even come out of her room. She stays in bed in the dark. We leave trays outside and she pulls them in as if she herself is sequestered. When the trays come out, hardly any of the food is gone. It's like my mother has become a bird. She picks at the corners of things, but doesn't eat much. So when I come downstairs, it's a bit of a surprise that today she made it all the way to the couch. She is screaming at my grandmother, who is sweeping the kitchen floor.

"Oh, leave me alone, Mom," my mother says; her voice is sharp in a way that hurts my ears.

"I'll leave you alone when you get off the couch and start acting like yourself again," Grandma Jackie says. "You're not the first woman in the world to have a life crisis."

My mom snaps and roars in response, as though Grandma Jackie's words are a sonic weapon, like Lady Bird's cry.

I walk slowly so that I won't be seen. But as small as I try to make myself, I'm caught.

"Where are you going?" my mom asks from the couch she's been sitting on since breakfast.

"Yuri Ross's," I say. "From school. A friend. We're hanging out."

She doesn't ask who Yuri is and what we're doing. I feel like before the events of this summer, she would ask me about him. Instead, she just grabs her car keys and says, "Let's go."

I'm so surprised that I follow her into the car.

She slides behind the wheel and starts the car and turns the satellite radio on. It's classical music, but she makes a sound with her throat like she's annoyed or going to throw up and then changes it over to a 1990s rock oldies channel.

A song comes on and she starts singing along immediately and banging the wheel in time.

While I give her directions, I just kind of look at her, as though she's an alien. Or been body-snatched. Wondering if she's becoming a friend or a foe.

She doesn't say anything. She just scream sings along to the songs that come up.

"Turn here," I say.

She drops me off at Yuri's house, which is not that far from us, but it's up a hill and walking up it is a killer.

"What time should I pick you up?" she asks, rolling down the window, calling after me.

"It's cool," I say, coming back and leaning into the car to talk to her. "I'll call a ride-share or something."

She looks too pale and fragile to be driving. And honestly, now that I see her, I'm afraid, probably like my grandma is, at her thinness. I shouldn't have let her drive me. She's not even really wearing proper clothes. I wonder if I should call Grandma Jackie to come get my mom.

"You should go get a gelato," I say, knowing that's her favorite dessert. "There's a place just down Hillhurst. Not too far from here."

She puts her hands on the steering wheel and looks off in the distance, but she's not really looking at anything. She just has a funny look in her eye. I think maybe she's losing it. Then she says the word *gelato*, rolls up the window, and drives away.

Well, I think. *Maybe it will be fine. She left the house.*

It's like Green Guarder said to the team when Gargantua left to be on her own. "First you are a seed. Then you germinate and bloom. Then you fruit. Only then, there is a moment when you have to decide to become sweet or bitter. And either way, you may rot on the vine or fall free. A million things and no guarantee."

I'm disappointed to see when I enter Yuri's living room that it is crowded with Phil and Tze jockeying for the console controller on the couch.

"Hey, Phil and Tze dropped by," Yuri says. He doesn't give me an extra look that says *I'm sorry* or anything; his eyes just kind of slide over me, not even noticing how cute I tried to look. It's kind of hard to read whether or not this was a date in the first place.

I try not to mind.

Phil and Tze might be there, but I notice that I am the only girl and that is definitely something. So I go with it. I settle into the couch next to Yuri. I sit really close to him.

We all start talking about *Yoll Castle*, the RPG game that I'm doing my second run-through of. The one where I am now totally evil.

"Oh, I'm playing that game," I say.

"You are?" Yuri asks. "You're a gamer girl?"

"Yeah, I just downloaded the new DLC, so I'm doing a second run-through."

"I just downloaded it, too," Yuri says.

"What's your character?" Phil asks.

Yuri boots up his console and he's a horseback-riding Knight in Shining Armor. All good and perfect and shiny. I can't help but think it's a little on the nose. I thought maybe he'd choose something a bit more interesting.

"I'm playing a rogue," I say. "Elf. Double daggers. Dark backstory. Lots of scars."

"Rogue is such a girl character to play," Phil says.

I don't mention that I've joined the assassins' league. I don't mention that my character is growing ugly from all the bad I'm doing. Also, rogues are thieves; you always have to have a thief in your party or you can't pick locks. A rogue is badass. They get right in there. They don't hide behind a horse or a shield or do magic from afar.

"I always do a run-through as everything with RPG games," I say. "To get the different stories. It's more fun that way."

"You play a Femme or a Male?" Tze asks.

"Most run-throughs as a Femme, but always once through as a dude to get the other story lines. I switch my race—elf, dwarf, human, or whatever," I say.

They all nod.

They don't offer up whether they ever play as a Femme. But I bet they do. There are games where you get to choose your gender, and games where you don't. And if you're a gamer, most play both. Sometimes, playing your opposite gender is a strategic choice. I bet Phil plays a girl just to look at her booty the whole time.

Yuri fires up his saved game and everyone starts taking turns playing, passing the controller from one to the other to have fair play. Except me. They never pass the controller to me. Even though I reach for it. I roll my eyes and settle back and watch. I know that there is a tricky puzzle coming up. It took me hours to figure it out. And I'm curious as to how they are going to fare.

When we get there, everyone is stumped. After watching them fumble for a bit, I pipe up.

"You have to shift the torches all to the left and then . . ." I say.

"We've got this," Yuri says, shushing me. I take it that he wants to figure it out on his own, but I notice that he doesn't seem to shush Phil and Tze when they give him ideas about how to conquer the puzzle. I don't like being shushed.

I watch for a little longer while they all continue to not get the puzzle.

"If you shift the torches to the left, then you can move that stone," I try again.

But they are talking and arguing amongst themselves about how to get through the puzzle. No one is listening to me. I sigh heavily, but no one hears.

"Ahhhh, this game is crap," Yuri says, throwing the controller onto the couch.

"Let's look at a walk-through," Tze suggests.

I pipe up again.

"If you shift the torches to the left, then when you move that stone, you'll find the key to the first cage under it," I say.

"Walk-throughs are lame," Yuri says.

"And for girls," Phil says.

"What?" I ask. Did he just say that? "For girls? I don't use a walk-through unless I am one hundred percent stuck. And so do you."

"Calm down," Phil says.

"I am calm," I say.

The boys look at me like they've suddenly noticed that I am with them. There's a weird tension in the room and I just want to say to Yuri, *kick them out so we can be alone*. But I don't. So we're all quiet except for the sound of the music of the game, and the clicking of the controller as Phil fails the puzzle and dies again. He throws the controller down and curses.

"I'm hungry," he says, changing the subject.

"Go put pizza in the microwave," Yuri says.

Phil and Tze head out of the room and Yuri scoots closer to me. I think he's going to apologize. He picks up my hand and holds it. My heart leaps.

"Sorry about the clowns. You having fun?" he asks.

"Sure," I say. But I'm kind of lying. It's not like watching on Twitch. It is not that fun to watch people play a game that you are better at playing than them. Especially when they don't listen to your advice. "I really like this game."

He looks at me and squints his eyes in a sexy kind of way.

"Wanna stay a little after everyone goes later?" he asks.

"Can you kick them out?" I say. "They are being obnoxious."

"Sure, after a few more quests, OK?" He scoots in a little closer to me. Yuri wants to be alone with me. With me. I can suffer through another annoying hour.

I nod.

"Cool," he says. "You're cool."

Then he lets go of my hand and squeezes my leg as he gets up, and it feels really nice.

"Do you want anything from the kitchen?" he asks.

"A juice box," I say.

He makes a finger gun at me and winks. I have to admit that sometimes I swoon a little bit at the way he looks. Ashy hair. Short on the side and curly on top. He looks like a hero from a story. But not like anyone from Team Tomorrow. I try to cast him as someone, but none of the characters quite fit.

He leaves the room and I can't help myself. I pick up the controller and restart from where all the boys died in the game. I move all the torches to the left, move the stone, get the key, and I open the first cage and keep going.

The boys walk back in and Yuri bumps me over from the center of the couch with his butt and grabs the controller from my hands as he hands me some juice. He doesn't thank me for getting past the part where they were all stuck.

Actually, none of them even mention it. They act as though they solved the puzzle themselves, and they forget that it must have been me. It could only have been me.

I am a little mad. I sit there stewing. I almost think I should just get up and leave. But I stay because I want to hang out with Yuri. Because I want him to be my first boyfriend. Finally, Yuri kicks Phil and Tze out and we are alone.

We're sitting on the couch together and the lights are kind of low.

"So, Edan, how'd you do the puzzle again?" he asks.

"Thank you for noticing," I say.

"Will you show me?"

I tell him how to solve the puzzle, and halfway through the telling, he pulls my face to him and kisses me.

It's slow and soft and nice. So I kiss him back.

"You are a real nerd," he whispers.

I know it's a high compliment.

Nine

I'm in the public library, the coolest refuge from the brutal heat wave currently hitting Los Angeles, and the cheapest place to hang out when you are on a zero budget.

I am also very glad to be out of the house.

I'm sitting at a table with a stack of costuming and sewing books when I notice a bunch of boys burst into the Teen Zone. I look up at them. They are too loud. They are laughing and throwing something around. Why is it that a group of boys together are sometimes so annoying?

I am flipping through the books on the history of costuming, trying to learn about pulling pieces together.

"*Shhhhhh.*" The YA librarian tells them to be quiet.

They laugh and slap one another on the back and start speaking in rapid Spanish that I can't understand even though I've been taking it in school. Laughing harder, they sink into their seats. They settle down by playing a board game that one of them pulls down from the games shelf.

I forget that they are there until I get up to grab a new book and pass the boys. One of them whistles at me and I freeze up. It's a wolf whistle and I don't like it. I tense up, trying to think of a comeback, but I'm slow at those sometimes, and by the time I come up with something, I hear another one of them say, "Hey, don't be like that."

I think he is talking to me, telling me not to be like that. So I turn around to tell him what's what. I'm ready to blurt a loud string of expletives, but when I'm facing them, it's obvious that the boy who said it is talking to his friend. Explaining how uncool that was. About how the friend should apologize to me. His friend looks up at me and mumbles a very low, and not quite genuine, "I'm sorry."

"Sorry about Juan," says the boy, who I realize with a start as I look closer at him is Kirk Gomez. "He can't help being an animal sometimes. But he'll learn."

His friend fake punches his arm and Kirk tousles him back in fun. It's really clear that they are good friends. They like each other, and I like that.

I don't want to say thank you or screw you. So I just kind of stand there and stare at them, like I'm a bit lost. I shake my head. Not up and down or side to side. Just a shake to acknowledge the apology but not accept or reject it.

Instead, what I'm really noticing is that there is something about Kirk Gomez that makes me uncomfortable. Like I'm close to a live wire and everything inside me is standing up at all ends.

"How was your show?" he asks.

I still am just standing there. Noticing that he is wearing an excellent *Yoll Castle* T-shirt. Noticing his dark eyes and how they are like drops of chocolate and how you can fall right into them and go swimming. I am swimming in his eyes. They go down very deep, like right down inside of him. I've been looking up close at Yuri's eyes for two weeks now, every time we kiss before I close my eyes, and they don't go that deep. How do eyes go that deep? How do they go so far down?

"It's Kirk Gomez," he says as though I don't know who he is. "I go to school with you. I saw you at Angeles Comic Con. I got you in."

"I know. I recognized you. It was fine," I say, shaking myself away from staring at him. Why did I say fine? I meant to say good. I meant to say great. "Thanks for getting me in."

"No problem," he says. "Are you doing summer school?"

"What?" I ask. Why does he make me feel like I am made of glass? Like he's seeing right through me. Like he knows that there is something wrong if I am here in the library, by myself, in the middle of the week in summer. That I should have something to do. Somewhere else to be.

"No, I'm not doing summer school," I say.

"There's no shame in that. I had to do summer school once. I failed science."

"I don't think it's shameful," I say. "But why would you think that?"

"'Cause you're so busy studying," his friend Juan says.

66

"You're just poring over those books over there like you are studying for your life. Respect."

It's true. I am. Maybe it *is* like I'm cramming for my life.

"I'm trying to learn a craft," I say to them. "I want to make a better Gargantua costume," I say directly to Kirk. Somehow I know he'll understand.

"Oh," Kirk says. "But you don't know how to sew?"

His friends cover their mouths and cough laugh and mumble something in Spanish, which I don't catch, into their hands.

"Not all girls know how to sew these days," I say, feeling angry. "I don't know what century you're living in."

Now his friends are laughing out loud. I am not understanding something, because there is no reason anyone should be laughing this hard. I steal a glance at Kirk to see if he's laughing, too. But Kirk is just calmly looking at his friends, his eyes narrow. He looks steely-eyed. And pissed. Then he looks back at me with a dead calm about him.

"I didn't ever say that," he says. "I live in this century."

I can tell that we both feel irritated, because there is that weird energy moving between us. Like it's buzzing, but now it's buzzing in all the wrong directions.

"I have to go," I say, and make my way over to the graphic novel section. I pull out a few tomes of Team Tomorrow. I figure I'll compare all the costumes and try to figure out which one is the easiest to start with. Start simple and work my way up.

When I get back to the teen section, Kirk and his friends are gone. And I'm glad of it. It's like the room feels a million times larger without them in it. But also as though there is a weird absence.

I settle back into my chair and I notice a book that wasn't there before on top of my stack. It's called *Sewing Made Simple* and as I flip through it, I see that it's a very clear and very easy to understand book. It's got a few simple patterns in it and there is a dress I think I could make. It's a good place to start.

"Thank you!" I say to the librarian, who looks up at me and shrugs.

"What?" she asks.

"Thank you!" I say. And I hold up the book. She smiles. So I smile back. She shrugs again and then goes back to doing something on her computer.

On page one of *Sewing Made Simple* it says, *"There are things that look simple that are hard. And there are things that look hard that are simple. But in both cases, you just have to follow the pattern."*

It's kind of like life.

TEAM TOMORROW

What is an ashcan?

In the golden age of comics, in order to establish copyright of a character and their powers, comic book companies would create a small pamphlet of a character with a sketch and a loose description of powers and backstory. This served to secure that character and state the company's proposed intention to print a story related to that character. Most printed only two copies, one for the Library of Congress and one for their records. Very few ashcans exist, as they were mostly thrown into the trash and were considered disposable.

The ashcan for Team Tomorrow is a small six-page pamphlet that has the original four team members and two villians. Only one badly water-damaged copy of this exists.

In modern comics, the ashcans are mini comics used mostly for promotional purposes such as a Who's Who of comics in an established company.

Ten

"So here's where we're at with SEW," I say.

"SEW?" Kasumi asks over Skype.

"Superheroes Everywhere," I say. "The name of our club."

"Because that's what we'll be," she says. "I like it. I don't know if some of the boys will like it."

"It's got the word *superhero* in it," I say. "They'll like it or else I'll use my superpowers to make them like it."

Kasumi laughs.

I click over to the online group that we started and check to see who has signed the official school club petition.

"Me, you, Yuri, Phil, Tze, Gwen and Joss Ferrar . . ."

I pause because I notice that there is a new name. It's Kirk Gomez.

"And Kirk Gomez."

"Cool, I don't even know some of those people," Kasumi says. "We're totally doing this. We're expanding our social circle."

"We're still two short," I say.

"We still have the rest of the summer," Kasumi says. "And we can recruit the first week of school. That's what Club Day is all about."

"True," I say. "But I worry that no one else will sign up and then we won't have a club."

"Since when did you become such a worrier?" Kasumi asks.

I didn't used to worry so much.

I worry that I still haven't told Kasumi what is going on with my family even though I almost have a million times. Not telling her kind of feels like it's not really happening.

Usually, I can talk to Kasumi about anything, and I still can, except I still haven't mentioned my father to her. She never brings it up and I think it's because she chalks it up to my being sad about my parents' fake breakup, and so she never mentions it, either. She does that because Kasumi is a good friend. Sometimes she even sends me articles about kids of divorce and stuff like that.

There is safety in the pixels and the thousands of miles between us, just like there is safety in being in a club. It forces group social interaction. And there is no better place to hide than in a group.

I worry that I am hiding.

Gargantua said that to Team Tomorrow when she left them. She thought they were all hiding. And she didn't want to hide anymore.

I change the subject.

"Who are you going to cosplay first?" I ask.

"I am really torn," Kasumi says. "There are so many to choose from. Sailor Moon? Star Wars? Anything Marvel? Maybe Kamala Khan. Maybe Phoenix? Shade, the Changing Girl?"

"Well, I thought we were prepping for Tomorrow Con to try to win the contest," I say. "So maybe you could try someone from Team Tomorrow. Lady Bird?"

Kasumi shrugs.

"I don't think I like Team Tomorrow as much as you do," she says.

"You know nothing," I say.

We both laugh. Then we start to talk about the *Game of Thrones* rewatch we are doing together over the summer. It's been a way for us to keep hanging out without actually being in the same city.

While we talk, I'm clicking around on Kirk's profile. I'm curious as to why he'd join the club. I am curious about him. I've been to the library again, and I've seen his friends sometimes, but I haven't seen him.

Kirk's profile is pretty locked down so that I can't really see anything. There's a profile picture and some general photos that don't tell me much.

"Edan!" Kasumi says. "Hello. What do you think?"

"What?"

"About who I should be first?" she asks. "Are you surfing while talking to me? Don't multitask!"

"Sorry, I was just looking at the pages at some of the kids who joined who we don't know."

"So what else is going on?" she asks. "What's happening with Yuri?"

"I'm not only hanging out with Yuri," I say. "I finally made out with Yuri."

Kasumi gets all excited, and her hands start flying around the video chat so fast that she just becomes little boxes because the streaming can't keep up with her movements. When she finally stops freaking out with joy for me, she leans super close into the camera.

"I could die," she says. "How was it?"

"Great," I say. "It's the one good thing about this summer."

"Junior year is going to be the best year ever," she says.

"It sure is," I say. And then I fake smile. It's easy to lie to your best friend when she's thousands of miles away. But what's going to happen when she's home and she realizes that my dad did not just separate from my mom?

"I gotta jet," I say as the weight of my world crushes down on me again.

Kasumi blows me a kiss and signs off. The image of her kissing me just hangs there on my monitor, and I keep the pic open for a minute because it's nice to have a friend who is happy and loving and not going through anything hard.

I move the window over a little and look at Kirk's page again. I bring the cursor to hover over the friend request button for a while. I feel weird about clicking it. I sit there rationalizing it in my head like a million different ways. Would it be weird if I friended him? Would he think we were friends? If he's going to be in my club, then I will have to be able to tag him. This really shouldn't be a big deal.

Finally, I click it. Friend request sent.

Two seconds later, Kirk Gomez accepts my friendship.

Eleven

I'm not myself right now. I don't recognize this person that I am. A person who goes and makes out with Yuri like it's going out of style. The one who locks herself in her room and slams doors. The one who lets her video game character become so evil that she betrays everyone in her party. The one who feels better as a supervillainess that is ten feet tall and scary-looking.

I put the fruit in the blender to make my smoothie as I contemplate.

"Take that mask off," Grandma Jackie says, entering the kitchen.

"I'm not wearing a mask," I say. I feel more like myself with it on.

She throws her hands up in the air and gives up.

"I'm going to have to go back to work soon," she says.

"So?"

"Why are you giving me attitude?" she says. "I don't need attitude. *We* don't need attitude."

"I'm not giving you attitude," I say. "This is my *personality*."

But it's not my personality.

There is something mighty powerful about wearing a mask. It gives you permission to be a version of yourself that you are not brave enough to be. It's you and it's also not you. When I'm wearing this mask, I feel like I can be myself a little bit. I can breathe.

"I know this is hard," Grandma Jackie says. "And I'm here for you. And for your mother."

"Do you have money to turn back on all the perks that I'm used to in life? Like an allowance. And a family?"

"That is a very narrow view of the world, Edan," she says. "I'm surprised at you."

"I feel like my world is narrow right now," I say. Like when Team Tomorrow got squeezed into a flat, two-dimensional, colorless world.

"We didn't have perks when I was growing up," she says.

"That's what all old people say."

"I don't feel that old."

"Well, you are."

She starts folding her napkin into a million tiny folds.

"I think that you should go outside and do something," she says, and I can tell from the way she says it that she's simmering. "I think you've been cooped up in this house too long and it's making you a bit crazy."

She thinks that outside will solve everything. Outside is the problem. Outside is expensive. Outside is bright when I feel dark. Outside is too much for me to handle.

"I'm going to play video games," I say, getting up from the table.

"GO OUTSIDE," she says. It is not a suggestion. It is a command.

"FINE!" I say, and I grab my sweater and bolt out the door.

I pick a direction and start walking. I walk and I walk and I walk and I walk.

I find myself at the Silver Lake Reservoir. There is a little park and people are picnicking and having lunch. Everyone is happy and laughing, with blankets spread out.

"You going to rob a bank? Or save the day?" I hear someone say.

I turn around. It's Kirk.

"Huh?" I say.

He points to my face.

I put my hand up and realize I forgot I was wearing a mask. I slowly lift the mask and take it off.

"You joined SEW," I say.

"I'm thinking of cosplaying Green Guarder," Kirk says.

"He's such a goody-goody," I say. But I squint and look him up and down. He'd make an OK Green Guarder.

"He's a hero," Kirk says. "The world could use that kind of hero, don't you think? Someone who is good and charitable, that everyone likes. That makes things bloom."

Standing there, I have a flash to being little and thinking that my dad was like that. He was a kind of hero to me. But underneath he was rotting.

"Heroes are for suckers," I say.

"I need that kind of hero," he mumbles.

"What?" I ask.

"M'ijo, does your friend want to join us? We've got extra," an older woman sitting with a woman wearing a hat calls out from a blanket, and Kirk turns to listen. They are beautiful and look a little bit punk rock. They've got sleeve tattoos and good eyebrows.

"It's a beautiful day, isn't it?" Kirk asks.

I look up at the sky and it is an impossible and beautiful blue. When I look back at him, he is looking down at his feet and doesn't say anything for a couple of minutes.

"My mom and grandma . . . We're having a picnic," he says, looking back at me.

I can't tell if he's inviting me to come join them or if he's just telling me what he's doing. It's confusing and I don't know how to react. He makes me feel weird. I'm trying to think of a way to say, *yeah, I'd like to sit for a minute.* But what if I am wrong and then I look foolish?

Silence becomes a shape that grows between us, becoming larger and more awkward as the time rolls by.

My phone buzzes and, relieved that I have something to do, I pull it out.

YURI: Hey. Come over. My parents are gone. ;)

"I gotta go," I say to Kirk. "I gotta meet someone."

He looks back up. His face looks weird. All screwed up and stuff. I show him the face of my phone so that he knows someone really texted me and I'm not lying.

"That works out. I kind of just want this picnic to be a family thing, but they'll insist that you come and sit with us," he says. "You understand, right? I'll tell them you had to go."

"OK," I say. It makes me feel weird, though. Like I'm being invited and rejected at the same time. It makes me feel crinkled inside, like I can't process things straight. But maybe that's just me and my state of being lately. Everything feels like it lands on me wrong.

"She has to go, she said next time," he calls back to them. The older woman smiles, nods, and the younger woman waves at me as though she knows me. As though I am really one of Kirk's friends.

"See ya," I say.

"See ya," he says.

I walk around the park until I hit Yuri's street. I look at the blue of the lake. The burst of the succulents. The crisp sky. The way my shadow falls exquisitely on the ground. It's me and it's not me.

The beauty. The beauty of a beautiful day that I can't truly see with a mask on.

Fall

HEROQUEST CON

One

The excitement of a new school year with a new wardrobe kind of falls flat. This year, there is no back-to-school shopping. Even doing odd jobs all summer didn't help. It just covered the cost of living. Not the cost of anything extra.

I do not get cute new clothes. I do not get new notebooks. My grandmother brings home some office supplies from the hospital so that I can replenish my school supplies stock a little bit. I know she means well, but it feels like it's rubbing the state of my life in my face.

It's not that new things are necessary for a new year. It's just that the action of getting a few new things heightens the anticipation. The ritual of shopping and picking things out usually makes me feel excited about a new year, and so the absence of doing those things makes me feel like Gargantua when she got stuck in one size and couldn't grow or shrink at all. It wasn't that being only one size was a terrible thing, it just was not what she was used to. What she was used to doing was taken away.

Having no marker for the end of summer and a new school

year, I mope around the house. Picking things up and putting them down. Moving from room to room, trying to find something to do. I hear the noises of the other women in the house moving around as well. We are like ghost ships missing each other in the mist. We haunt this space, mapping out the geography of our sadness.

"You've got a letter," my mom calls from the other room. I rarely see her anymore. I just hear her random movements.

When I enter the room, she's there, but it's also like she's gone.

I want to grow Gargantuan and use her mass powers to make my mom seem less translucent and more whole. But when I look at her and give her my best superhero flare glare, she looks back at me and I am so sad that I swallow my rage.

"Thanks," I say.

She hovers for a moment, and then sort of glides out of the room.

The letter is propped up by the vase that no longer holds flowers like it used to because flowers are an extravagance that cannot be afforded. Even though they cheer up a room. Even if they cheer me.

Who am I kidding? Not even flowers can cheer me. They didn't work on Gargantua. Her garden died.

No one really writes letters anymore. I haven't received many letters in my life. But I like the *idea* of letters. It's a shame that mostly what comes for me in the mail is just nonsense or junk or school stuff or the occasional birthday card.

But this is a genuine letter.

From my dad.

Dear Edan,

Thank you for the package of books. I really appreciated them. I was glad that you sent me Team Tomorrow: Tomorrow Is Today V.1 and 2. It was interesting! I really connected with Lady Bird. Maybe because she flew so high and then was grounded and had to spend all that time with broken wings. She has a lot of recovering to do. I am feeling like her—a bit bruised. Pretty great that a comic book can give you a new perspective on your own life. Things here are about as you expect. It's hard. I miss my life. I miss the Internet. I miss you and your mom. I hope you'll visit next time.

Send me more comics. They really help to pass the time.

Looks like there will be a trial. Hopefully it will all get sorted out and I'll be cleared.

I hope to be home soon.
Dad

I don't know when I started crying. If it was at the beginning of the letter or the end of it.

I drop the paper on the table and just keep pushing at my eyes, and I can't see anything because there are too many tears. It's crazy how sometimes deep, deep crying is so quiet. You'd think it would be loud. But instead, it's like you are gasping for air and you are leaking all over the place. Eyes, nose, pits.

"You all right?" my grandmother says, coming into the room. She is readying herself for her rounds at the hospital.

I shake my head from side to side to say no. No. NO. NO! NO!

She puts her bag on the table and comes over to me and pulls me into her arms. She whispers to me and rubs my back. I don't even hear everything she's saying, but her words still sink and seep so far down inside that they spread into all the cracks and breaks I have. They fill and expand. And it's the *soothing* that is the most painful. The painful truth that hurt *hurts* and that there is no stopping the hurt. It has to do its thing and you have to live through it. She is whispering love to me and rubbing hope into my back with her strong hands and holding me tight with arms that love me.

"I have to go, Edan," she says after a bit. "Are you going to be all right?"

I want to say I won't ever be all right. The path I thought was forward is gone. It's just walls everywhere. Will I be able to go to college? Will my life ever feel as though it is mine again? What's going to happen to us if my father doesn't come back home?

But I don't say that. Instead, I wail, "I don't have any new clothes for school!"

Which is the dumbest thing I could ever say because it's not what I want to say at all. But it's what comes up first. It's what is safe to say, because everything else is too large to deal with. No new clothes is a problem that can be attacked. It can be named. It can even possibly be solved.

"What about all of those sewing projects you've been doing?" Grandma Jackie says. "Those ugly costumes you insist on wearing to dinner."

"My cosplay?" I say. "Gargantua?"

I almost laugh at the idea of wearing a skintight royal purple unitard with fake leather squares and a capelet to the first day of school. I imagine how the capelet will go over when I'm sitting in math class. Maybe instead of a silver G on my chest, I could wear an E for Edan.

That makes me crack a smile.

"Seems to me if you can sew those up, you can do something for yourself. Maybe alter something old to make something new?"

And just like that, my tears that flowed as though they would never stop, stop.

"I never thought about that," I say. My mind is whirring.

Gram kisses my forehead and pats my arm and leaves the house. She's going to go to the hospital and do surgery in the pediatric ward on a little girl. She's always been a real-life hero.

As soon as she shuts the door, I go upstairs and pull everything I own out of my closet and all of the bags that my mother had gathered up to get rid of. I take these things and I sort through. I do as that lady said: Hug the clothes and feel them. If they give you joy, if they look like they want to be turned into something else . . . keep them.

If they don't, they go into the discard pile.

When I am done, the keeper pile is all potential. I take the items and I begin.

I rip and stitch. I cut and darn. I alter and flair.

I do the best job I can with my limited skills.

Everything is the same, but it is also a bit different.

Two

asumi has been back for three days, but she is too jet-lagged to hang out right away.

Let me come over, she texts. *I'm finally back in this time zone.*

My house too toxic, I text back. *Your house, please.*

I don't want to be at my house. I don't want her to see the way I live now. Where my mom doesn't even bother to hide her puffy eyes or put on clean clothes. Where my grandmother makes dinners that I don't like and we barely talk. Where the house is messy and the plants are dying. Where I stare at my feet all the time because I can't look anyone in the eyes. Where we talk about some things but not about it.

I don't want to talk about it.

I pack a bag with pajamas and stuff and am almost giddy with the thought of being out of the house for a whole twenty-four hours.

"You're going to see Kasumi?" my mom asks as she stands in the kitchen and sorts through the boxes of tea in the cupboard.

"Yeah," I say. "She's back from Japan. Her dad was shooting a new film."

I can't trust that my mom remembers anything anymore. She's not paying attention like she used to.

"He's in the cinematographers guild," my mom says, more to herself than to me.

"Yeah, I guess," I say. "He's a *cinematographer*. I don't really keep track of what unions people are in."

"No," she says. "Why would you?"

"So I'm going to go," I say.

"You know, I used to put together a lot of feature film projects," she says. "Hollywood is like a living organism. If one part is rotten, you have to cut it off to save the rest."

I stand there for a minute. I look from side to side. I look at her. She's looking at me and then suddenly I am crossing the room in long steps. As though my legs are long and can cross vast amounts of space quickly like Gargantua does when she grows tall. Then my arms are suddenly long and stretching out from me and they land square on the shoulders of my mom. And even though I am shorter than she is, I feel as though I'm almost looking down at her.

"You could put projects together again," I say. "You have the power."

I say it with a voice that I don't even know I have.

She leans back against the counter and her shoulders sink. But my hands are on her like magnets lifting her up. I am determined to not let her sink. Still, she does.

"I don't think I can," my mom says so softly that I barely hear it.

I have no power here.

"Do you need a ride?" my grandmother says. I wonder how long she's been there, watching us.

"That'd be nice," I say.

"Let's go," she says, and I start to follow her. Gram pauses at the kitchen door and turns back to my mom, who is still leaning against the sink. "How about you unload the dishwasher while I'm gone. My shoulder is acting up and I've got surgery tomorrow."

My mom nods so slightly that we can barely see it.

"Good," Grandma Jackie says, and we head outside.

"Which part is the lie?" I ask my grandmother when we get to the car. "The shoulder or the surgery?"

"The shoulder," she says.

It's kind of like she used a psychic ray on my mother just like I tried to use my gargantuan strength. I don't know that either of us won this round.

When Kasumi opens the door and says hello, for one brief moment I feel at peace.

Mr. and Mrs. Takata look weary and worried. I assume it's jet lag. But Kasumi looks bright and cheerful and she's wearing a fabulous new outfit that you could never get here.

"Hi!" she says excitedly. And we both rush into each other's arms. And maybe I hold her in a hug for a just a bit longer than I normally would, because I need this hug. Even if you can't really say anything with your mouth, a hug says, *I'm here. I'm here. No worries with whatever ails you. I'm here.*

"So," I say.

"So," she says.

"Should I show you the things that I bought?" Kasumi asks.

"Yeah," I say.

She holds up each item from her still-unpacked suitcase. I squirm in the chair, not really wanting to see everything. And also thinking that some of the things she thinks are cute and cool, I don't think are.

"Maybe let's see some pictures," I say.

I move over to the bed and we scroll through the pictures on her tablet. She is a real pro when it comes to pictures. There are cityscapes and gardens and temples and film set pictures and family pictures and bullet train pictures and cat cafés and, really, looking at too many pictures of someone else's good time is not so fun, and the best ones I already saw and liked on social media.

Worse. It reminds me of all the pictures I didn't take of things that I didn't do.

"How about you?" she asks. "Show me your pictures."

"I don't have many," I say. I pull out my phone and I show her a couple of pictures of me and Yuri kissing.

"Nice," she says.

I scroll back not that much further because there wasn't really much to take of my life this summer.

"Oh, this is good," I say. And I show her pictures that I took of the cosplayers at Angeles Comic Con.

"Wow," Kasumi says. "Some of these costumes are great."

"Yeah," I say. "Look."

I show her the pictures I took of the Team Tomorrow panel. But they are kind of far away, so I pinch the picture to widen one of them that is the most clear. I zoom right into the actress who is playing Gargantua.

"She's perfect," Kasumi says. "I can't believe you were there."

But I don't answer her at first. Because as I zoomed, I notice that right in the front row is Kirk. He's frozen and staring at the actors, his hands up over his head like he is reaching out to touch them. He is such a fanboy. It makes me smile to myself.

I am still looking at the picture, but Kasumi has moved on and she's flitting around the room like a bird and then she is hungry, so we go downstairs.

As we delve deeper in the catch-up, I find that I am holding back and it's as though there is a barrier between us. It's like things are weird for some reason. Like there is a distance between us that I can't quite articulate. We're off balance. We're out of sync.

She says, "Do you want to go out?" just as I say, "Let's stay in?"

"You go first." "You go first."

"Hungry? Food?" "So full. Movie?"

We stutter and start. Everything seems the same as before but different. I feel like we're underwater and everything is distorted.

Is it her? Is it me? Have we grown apart during the summer? Sometimes that happens with friendships.

We're not the way we used to be because I am an island and there is no way to get to me. It's a bit like what Gargantua does when she splits off from Team Tomorrow. She grows so big that they can't talk to her anymore. And after a period of silence, she leaves.

Who am I kidding. I *know* the problem is me. I've changed. Worry and weariness have changed me. The world isn't fun right now. It's like a heavy wet blanket. And it's hard to explain that to someone for whom things are just the same as before. It's like she's moved forward a few steps and I've been dragged back. Like we are living in different time streams.

Sure, we can still talk; there is always stuff to say even when there is nothing to say. I tell her about Yuri. But when it comes to the things I really want to talk about, and my awful situation, I stall out. I sputter. I become silent.

As the night goes on, we finally get on the same page and I chalk everything up to just having been away from each other for a couple of months. We sit in silence, finishing our binge watching of *Game of Thrones* that we started over the summer. Before we go to sleep, I think to myself that it's not too late to tell her everything. And I know if I don't tell her soon, it will be.

At 1:00 a.m., I wake up. My stomach feels sick. It's not from too much ice cream mochi that I had. It's like a deep pit of dread inside me.

"I don't feel well," I say, waking her up.

"You can go be sick," she says, pointing to the bathroom. "I'll go in another room if you want privacy."

I shake my head. This overwhelming sense that I have to get out of here overcomes me.

"No, I want to go home," I say. "I think I should go home."

Kasumi uncurls herself from her bed and goes into the hall. I can hear her talking in Japanese to her dad, who then comes into the room.

"Do you need a doctor?" he asks.

"No," I say, almost wanting to cry because it's so nice that someone might think I need something. "I just really don't feel well."

Mr. Takata nods.

"I'll take you home," he says. "I'm still not on LA time."

He did that for me once before at my first sleepover with Kasumi, when I was nine. I woke up, just like this, in the middle of the night, confused that I wasn't in my own room. The door was in the wrong place. The window looked like it was on the ceiling. The floor was hard. I started to cry and Kasumi went and woke up her dad, who threw a robe on and drove me home. It had never happened again, until now.

I felt like my nine-year-old self, sitting in the backseat of the car with Kasumi, who insisted on coming with us and was fussing over me the way you do when you care about someone. I wish she hadn't come along so that I could just feel bad all by myself. But friends stick with friends.

"Oh my gosh," I say to myself but loud enough to be heard.

"What is it?" Kasumi asks. "Are you going to puke? Dad, Edan is going to puke."

"Should I pull over?" Mr. Takata asks.

"No," I say. "I'm fine. It's that guy, Kirk Gomez, who joined our SEW club."

Kasumi looks out the window. There, walking down the street, fists in hoodie pockets, is Kirk Gomez.

"Oh, yeah," Kasumi says. "I remember him now. He was in one of my classes. Nice guy."

"Yeah," I say. "He helped me get into Angeles Comic Con this summer."

"He was in my math class," Kasumi says.

We have moved past him, but we both turn and look out the back window. He becomes smaller and smaller until the night swallows him up.

"Do you think he needs a ride?" Kasumi asks. Nice Kasumi. Wonderful Kasumi. She starts to lean forward to tap her dad and make him go back for Kirk.

"I think he wants to be alone," I say.

I don't know that. But I know from the way he was walking that he had something big on his mind. I recognize the way he walks because I recognize it in me.

Whatever it is that he's carrying on his shoulders, it weighs heavy.

TEAM TOMORROW

When Gargantua left Team Tomorrow to work against them, the person she betrayed the most was Green Guarder.

Script

ISSUE 44

Page 1, Panel 1
Extreme close-up of Gargantua, looking like a woman in a Lichtenstein painting. She is crying and there is rain.
GARGANTUA: I CAN'T EXPLAIN WHY I'M LEAVING. MAYBE I'M JUST BAD.

Page 1, Panel 2
We widen out to see Gargantua towering over a cowering Green Guarder. He is spent from the battle they just had. The vines that grow from him, withering. Brown and yellow.
GREEN GUARDER: I CAN MAKE ANYTHING BLOOM. IT'S MY GIFT. EVEN YOU.
GARGANTUA: SAY GOOD-BYE, GUARDER. WE WON'T BE SEEING EACH OTHER AGAIN.

Page 1, Panel 3
We are focused on Green Guarder in the rain. He's looking up, presumably at Gargantua.
GREEN GUARDER: WE'LL MEET AGAIN. YOU CAN COUNT ON IT.

Page 1, Panel 4
Long shot of Green Guarder using all his green spell to throw one last vine out at a retreating Gargantua. We can see that there is a single purple bloom on the end. He is giving it to her as a gift.

Page 1, Panel 5
It is a close-up of Gargantua's boot, crushing the purple flower.
CAPTION: SHE WOULD REGRET CRUSHING THAT FLOWER. BUT NOT TODAY.

Three

Despite everything that is going on in my personal life, there is a feeling you get that anything is possible the first week of school. Like the whole year stretches out in front of you and it could all be different. *Better*. Even my circumstances, or my repurposed wardrobe, can't change that excited feeling that the year is a blank slate.

Kasumi and I have almost no classes together this year. But we do have the same lunch period, which is more than nothing. Maybe even better. Because you can't hang out in class.

Week one is always settling into the schedule. It's like immersing yourself in the infinite possibilities. Not unlike when Team Tomorrow had all those adventures when they fought the villain Time Stream and they visited all of the possibilities that could have occurred after the moment of the epic battle. All of those parallel worlds. All of those choices that they didn't take.

Right now, from week one, I am like Team Tomorrow and

I can clearly see how everything in my path for this year could go either way. And I'm rooting for the good way.

During nutrition, I can't help but have a bit of a spring in my step. I've gotten all the paperwork in for SEW and I'm headed back from the office, having completed club sign-up day. But as I'm walking across the quad, out of the corner of my eye, I see something happening.

There are two boys who look as though they are dancing.

I slow my gait.

They are not dancing. They are scuffling. They are pulling on each other's hoodies and pushing each other and pulling each other apart.

Technically they are not fighting. They are wrestling. They are trying very hard to not throw punches. But they are hurling curses at each other. Their shirts are pulled out of their pants. I see skin. They fall to the ground and I stop.

One of the boys on the ground is Kirk. The other is his friend Juan.

They roll away from each other. They curse some more.

"Break it up." The teacher comes over.

"We're just playing," I hear Kirk say.

"You can tell me all about it in the office," the teacher says. "Both of you. Now. We gotta call your parents."

"Please don't call my mom," Kirk says. He sounds really upset about it.

"If you don't want me to call your parents, then don't rough-house at school. You know the rules," the teacher says.

"I'm sorry, man," Juan says to Kirk, and then puts his arm around him. It's shockingly tender after the way they were going at each other.

"Let's go, boys," the teacher says.

They both curse again and then follow the teacher into the bowels of the administration wing of the school.

As they pass by me, Kirk gives me a long look that says, *I'm one scuffle away from losing it.*

Another face comes into view after he's gone.

"Hey." It's Yuri smiling at me.

It takes me a moment to adjust to him. Yuri's face looks flat and two-dimensional after the intensity of Kirk's look.

I must be looking intense as well.

"I like it when you look at me like that," he says, looping his arm around me. He said he would meet me at the quad this morning and here he is, thinking I was looking for him.

"Spot me for a chocolate milk?" he says.

I don't tell him I wasn't looking at him, or for him, or thinking about him. Because I had forgotten all about him.

But I just kiss him and then I just give him the money for the vending machine that I can't afford to give.

four

wo weeks later, it's our first official SEW meeting and
everyone comes in costume. We are fourteen people
hanging out after school, resplendent in spandex.

I look around and take in the many colors and superhero/
sci-fi/fantasy symbols, sigils, and emblems and all of the feath-
ers, glitter, satin, and leather.

I am a noob and so is pretty much everyone else. Joss and
Gwen, the Ferrar twins, have cosplayed before, but just dab-
bled. Nothing serious. But even though I am new to all of this,
I can already tell just from wearing my own thrown-together
Gargantua costume that it takes a certain amount of bravery
to put forward the character that you connect with. It's like
exposing something secret about yourself. There is something
powerful about changing out of who you are into who you wish
you were. It's like a part of you is more you than just you in jeans
and a T-shirt.

One thing for sure is that it's fun to pack your schoolbag
with a superhero cape (well, capelet). It makes me feel I have

the opposite of a secret identity. Like when I took my costume out of my backpack, I became more me.

It was Kasumi's idea that we come dressed up. She thought that we'd be able to see what kinds of styles we were dealing with and what levels of craft. That it would set the tone of the club. That way we would immediately not feel self-conscious in front of one another when we made our new costumes, if we were covered up with masks and cloaks or were wearing nearly nothing at all.

Our club meeting takes place inside the costume room, which was assigned to us by the main office. It is a few doors down from the auditorium and is used by the theater club and stage crew, and they are not happy about having to share. But it's a room with large tables and sewing machines and lots of clothing racks.

The stage crew needs to just deal with it.

I wait a bit after we're supposed to start, to let stragglers arrive and people sort of mingle for a bit. Then I step out in front of the club and lift my chin, wearing the costume that I'd worked on all summer. It's from the Silver Age run of Team Tomorrow. Where Gargantua wears kicky boots and a capelet. There are patterned *T*s on the costume from when the team wore a uniform. I really own it. I feel as tall and powerful as Gargantua.

"Welcome to SEW: Superheroes Everywhere," I say.

"We're not all superheroes," Phil shouts out.

"It's just an acronym," I say. "It has *sew* in it, get it?"

"I don't really sew," Gwen says, raising her hand. A bunch of other people kind of mumble and nod.

"Well, it's the spirit of it," Kasumi says, backing me up. "Crafting your costume."

"Exactly," I say, grateful for the thread to follow. "We're all at different levels and have different skills. I know that I want to learn how to make stuff. But other people might just want to dress up. Can we agree that our club is about cosplaying, no matter how we get there? Crafting ourselves, store-bought, closet cosplay, or custom-made, all are acceptable here."

Everyone nods.

I take a deep breath and mentally cross off the first agenda item on my club list.

"OK. As I posted on our official club board, HeroQuest Con is this Thanksgiving. And I think that should be our goal for debuting our first costumes."

Every con has its little quirk. HeroQuest Con is a smallish-size con that prides itself as focusing on characters from across all franchises and media. Rather than keep the properties separate, they divide things up by archetype. Its focus on characters and encouragement of cosplay makes it a perfect first con outing for our club.

Everyone murmurs in agreement that it gives us a good date to aim for to get our cosplay projects finished.

"All in favor, say aye." I hold up my hand.

"We have consensus," Kasumi says.

"So now that we are agreed, I propose that the first order of business is that everyone signs up to get their badge now," I say. I have learned my lesson. I did the research. Nerdy things sell out fast. Being a nerd is no longer a rare or outsider thing; only being your particular kind of nerd is. Being a nerd is mainstream with hard-core nerd edges. Which means the modern nerd has to be prepared to be the early-bird nerd in order to not miss the nerd train.

I point to the computer behind me. "I've opened it up to the registration page. It's seventy-five dollars for the weekend."

I hear a few swears and mutters under the breath. I know how they feel. It took me a while to save up that much money this summer. It wasn't fun. I pulled up weeds. I babysat kids I didn't like. But I had a goal in mind besides the occasional latte and movie: a HeroQuest Con badge and reams of fabric to make my cosplay dreams come true.

"Do we have to go?" Gwen pipes up in the back. She's wearing a cobbled-together Black Widow outfit and she is rocking it.

"No," I say. "But it will be fun to go as a group."

"Maybe we can set up a scholarship," Yuri says. "You know, a fund for the group. We're a club, right? We have dues?"

I look at Yuri and smile. That's who I've been kissing all summer and a little part of my heart kind of swoons. I like that he's come up with a solution.

"Yes!" I say. "That's a great idea. We can do a booster for our club. It can pay for shared costume supplies and registration for those who are having trouble."

People like me. I will probably need help for the next thing we do. They don't know it, but I need all the help I can get. I push that out of my head and concentrate on the task at hand and go about other club business, like voting for club positions. In the end, I am elected club president. Joss is vice president. Kasumi is secretary. Yuri is treasurer. We bandy about ideas for fund-raising. Bake sales. Car washes. Dues.

The time goes by fast, and out of the corner of my eye, I see a girl from the costume department hovering by the door and giving me an annoyed glare. She's a small, curvy black girl.

"You have to hurry up," she says. "I need to be in here."

"We get two hours once every two weeks in here," I say to her. "Cut us some slack."

"Edan." Kasumi gives me a glare. "Come in, Sophie, and get what you need."

She shakes her head and rolls her eyes, grabs what she wants, and goes back outside.

"They do kind of own this room," Kasumi says.

"I know," I say. "But we are allowed a little corner."

"I'll go talk to her," Kasumi says. "She's in my English class. We're friends."

Kasumi goes to the doorway and starts talking to Sophie. In no time at all, as is Kasumi's way, she has the girl laughing at something and I know we're going to be OK.

While she's still smoothing things over with Sophie, I get an idea. I start to pull costumes off of one rack and load them onto another.

"Sophie says it's cool, she'll teach me how to use these machines during our free period so I can pass the info along. And basically just don't break anything, and respect the schedule," Kasumi says when she comes back into the room. "Wait. What are you doing?"

"We need our own costume rack," I say.

I take a Sharpie and scrawl on a hanger, *SEW CLUB*.

"They are not going to pay attention to that," Kirk says.

He's right. They won't. We need to occupy the space. Claim it in some way. I get an idea.

"Everybody, step out of your costume and come hang something up on this rack," I say.

I start. I peel off my capelet. I am standing there in my mask, fishnets, and a bodysuit, when I hear some of the boys wolf whistling. It doesn't make me feel good or sexy, and I hesitate. What am I doing?

"We just need a few pieces on there. Not everything," I say.

"I'll take inventory," Kasumi says, donning her secretary duties and doing an intake on a spreadsheet on her tablet.

"And can I make a motion?" Kirk pipes up, flashing me his dark eyes.

"Go ahead," I say, blushing a little. Why am I blushing?

"No whistling," Kirk says.

"I second that," Gwen and Joss say at the same time.

"When I see something sexy, I call it out," Phil says.

"It's not cool," Kirk says.

Every girl in the club nods emphatically.

"My girl *is* sexy," Yuri says.

"I'm not saying she isn't," Kirk says. "I'm just saying let's not objectify girls in front of everyone."

Did Kirk just say I was sexy?

"What are you? Some kind of social justice warrior? When I see sexy, I say sexy," Phil repeats. "How about boys? Can we whistle at boys?"

"Come on, Phil," Yuri says, pulling at his friend. But laughing, too.

"You have a girlfriend now and you're a bit whipped, aren't you?" Phil says. "Man up."

Yuri stops laughing and starts to go for Phil, but Kirk steps between them and calmly puts his hands on both boys' chests.

"Enough," Kirk says. "Don't mess up things for the club by fighting. They're strict about horseplay."

I remember seeing Kirk on the floor with Juan, trying hard not to fight, but very obviously wanting to fight. I wonder what happened when they went to the office, what were the consequences that I couldn't see? What would the consequences be if our faculty advisor stopped by to check in on us and saw this? Would we be disbanded before we even started?

All I know is that I saw Kirk and Juan laughing together the next day coming off the bus, like nothing had happened. Friends fight and friends come back together.

"Let me go," Yuri says. "This doesn't concern you."

There is a kind of spark between Yuri and Kirk as they size each other up. Like a hot live wire that rubs the wrong way. You can feel the ripple of dislike pass back and forth between them. It makes me feel both excited and also embarrassed. And from the way he's coiled up, I bet Kirk could hurt Yuri. And then he'd get in real trouble.

I step between them to cut off the current.

"Just don't do it," I say to everyone. "Don't whistle. It's kind of weird and we might be in different states of undress in this club, so let's keep it cool."

"I quit," Phil says, and storms out of the room. Tze looks at Yuri and they give each other a look, and then Tze nods and shrugs and follows Phil out the door.

"Ugh. Boys and their pissing contests," Kasumi says. "Another reason I'm so glad I don't like them."

"OK." Sophie, the costume girl comes in. "I'm coming in now."

The moment deflates and Yuri shrugs. Kirk slaps him on the shoulder and everything seems like it's suddenly all right between them.

I pull my jeans and T-shirt out of my bag and move to put them on, and as I do I glance at Kirk. Kirk looks at me and points to a far corner of the room. I look over there and see a shade for dressing behind. I move behind it.

"Didn't take us all for prudes," I overhear Yuri say, like he's a bit bitter about everything.

"I'm not," I hear Nadine say.

I hear a bunch of snorts and laughs.

I'm fully dressed now and when I emerge, Yuri loops his arm through mine. And even though he is my boyfriend and I want him to show it off to everyone, it feels kind of possessive. I slide my arm out from his and let it drop to my side. My own person. Not possessed.

I shoot a glance over at Kirk, who is no longer paying attention to me or to Yuri. He's laughing in the corner with Nadine. I feel a little twist inside about that, but I shake it off. He can hang out with Nadine. Nadine is cool.

"Let's go get some tacos," Yuri whispers in my ear. I snap my heart back to being a twosome.

When we get to the car and I'm waiting for Yuri to unlock my side of the car, he stops, hesitating by his car door, looking at me funny.

"You going to go like that?" he says. "Isn't that taking it a bit far?"

"What?" I say. "I changed. I'm a girl, no longer a supervillain."

He points to his eyes. "You left your mask on."

"Did I?" I say and touch my face. And I connect with the hard plastic that is most definitely not my face.

I lift it off and get in the car and place it on my lap.

Why, without it on, do I feel so naked?

TEAM TOMORROW

In issue 1, all the stars of Team Tomorrow have been working independently, thinking they are alone in a world of normal humans. Gargantua grows. Green Guarder drinks in the sun and makes things bloom. Figment retells the way you remember the story. Magnetic Pole changes north.

When Shock, another hidden super, suddenly comes into her powers, she goes on a rampage of Tower City. These individual heroes decide to come out from hiding to save their city. When they arrive at the street that Shock is attacking, they are each surprised to find others with special powers like themselves. Recognizing that they are not alone, Gargantua, Green Guarder, Figment, and Magnetic Pole rush in from the four different city corners they are standing on and work together to fight a common enemy.

The comic panels work very well, as they carefully separate all of the heroes that would become Team Tomorrow for the entire issue, showing their individual strengths. Each character gets to star alone. Even in the final battle, not one of them is ever in the same panel together, but somehow, the panel separation makes them seem completely together. It's not until the final splash page, when they subdue Shock and save the city, they all finally join one another in the middle of a destroyed Tower City Block.

It was a clever way to show a team coming together.

five

SEW's first group outing is a midnight movie.

Opening-night midnight movies are no longer at midnight. They are at 7:00 p.m. So when I tell Grandma Jackie, who is the only one who cares about my comings and goings right now, that I'm going to the opening of a new Star Trek movie with my friends, to the midnight screening, it's a lot easier for her to say yes after saying no.

Star Trek is not my thing. I mean, it's OK, but the Ferrar twins, Joss and Gwen, are totally into it. It's their favorite. One thing I like about being a nerd is that everyone has a favorite thing. And to them it's the best. And they can stand and argue and count and list the ways that it is the best. And every nerdy thing is always the winner because everyone can argue and back up the reasons that it is the best.

The answer is always the same. EVERY. THING. IS. THE. BEST.

Here is the truth about being a nerd. You don't have to

be an expert in something, you just have to be passionate. There is no test and no application. Only love of a thing that is the best.

This week the best is Star Trek. The new Star Trek movie is out and so it is automatically the winner. Next week the best will be something else.

But of course the real reason why I'm totally cool with the movie choice is because it means we'll get to see the debut of the *Team Tomorrow* trailer. Sure, I could have already watched it this morning when it dropped online. But I decided that I wanted my first viewing of it to be on the big screen. I can watch a million times later on my phone.

"Club rules! Everyone has to come cosplaying someone from the movie," I say.

"But Star Trek is so . . ." Nadine says.

"White," Kasumi says. "Not really a lot of people to play from the original series."

"Well," the Ferrar twins pipe up at the exact same time in the freaky way they do. "How about it's just from any version of Star Trek . . ." Joss says.

"That opens it up a lot," Gwen says, finishing the thought.

We put it to a vote and then agree. Any Star Trek is acceptable.

With the first of our club money, Yuri, as treasurer, orders a block of tickets at a theater with a huge screen and we get good seats.

"Hey," Yuri says, counting up the money he has in his hands that he got as cash. "Can you have people who don't have cash PayPal you, and then you give me the cash?"

"They can just PayPal you directly," I say.

"I know; my account was hacked and is messed up right now," he says.

"OK," I say, and give out my email to people and make a mental note to give Yuri the cash later.

Now I'm standing with Kasumi outside the movie theater. The Santa Ana winds have kicked up, so it's pretty blustery. Kasumi is dressed as a B'Elanna Torres. She used wax to make her forehead ridges and it looks good but a little weird.

"Your forehead is wonky," I say.

"I'm having trouble with the glue," Kasumi says. "Makeup is hard."

"Maybe we should make that one of our club activities? Watch a bunch of makeup videos on YouTube?"

"Good idea," Kasumi says. "The makeup doesn't blend so well from my skin to the wax, I think."

"We live in Hollywood; maybe there is some kind of makeup studio tour that we can take?" I say as I press on her forehead and nose, trying to make it a bit better.

"I'll ask my dad," Kasumi says. "He must know someone."

"Also, I thought maybe we could take portraits of us as our characters," I say. "I think that would be a cool activity and you could take the pictures. What do you think?"

"That's great," Kasumi says. "I've seen a bunch of cosplay photo shoots online that I can get inspiritation from."

I'm dressed up as Yeoman Rand, because an old-school Star Trek outfit was easier to pull together. Although, as I'm quickly learning with cosplay, not that easy. I understand why people order custom-made costumes. There are delicate subtle things that make a costume leap to the next level. Like the exact cut of the minidress. Mine is a little sloppy. I altered it from a dress I found at a thrift shop. It passes, but I still need to get better with the patterns and the sewing machine. My stitching sucks.

And I really have to start stepping up my thrifting game for pieces.

The Ferrar twins arrive first. Gwen is Spock and Joss is Deanna Troi. I have to say that they look pretty great and I had to stop for a second because it took me a moment to realize that they gender-swapped.

"You both look so fantastic," I say.

"We know," they say in unison.

I hand them two tickets next to each other.

Spock puts up his hand to stop me.

"Just 'cause we're twins doesn't mean we want to sit next to each other," they say at the exact same time, like they are one person.

I take a ticket back and swap it out.

"I thought we weren't going to do that," Kasumi says.

"I can't fight them," I say. "Spock used his Jedi mind trick on me."

"I think you mean the Vulcan mind meld," Kasumi says. "They have to touch your face to do it."

"You know what I mean," I say. And we laugh about crossing the nerd streams.

Slowly, other people show up and I hand out the tickets. We pretty much agree that it's first come, first served, but I'm holding one ticket back next to mine for Yuri so we can be together.

"Where is he?" I mutter under my breath.

"He'll show," Kasumi says.

"I feel weird holding all this cash for him," I say. "I just want to give it to him already."

I stand there, scanning every face that makes its way up to the box office, looking for someone familiar. Finally, I notice someone, but it's not Yuri I see strutting toward me. It's Kirk.

He's wearing a gold shirt. He's got his hair slicked back, 1960s style. He tugs on his shirt and saunters up to me like the real Captain Kirk hitting on a yeoman. A little part of me kind of tingles. He doesn't look like himself. He looks different.

"Hello, Yeoman Rand," he says, knowing exactly who I am.

"Captain Kirk," I say, handing him one of the last tickets.

"Worst job ever, besides captain of a starship," Kirk says. "Standing outside waiting for stragglers."

"Worst," Kasumi says.

Kirk's right. Everyone else is socializing in the lobby and we're out here freezing and being responsible. The holdup is that Yuri and his posse are late. I'm learning that he is always late. It's a bit irritating. It's one of his flaws.

But unlike the others, Kirk doesn't go inside the lobby to get out of the wind and talk to the others in SEW. He lingers outside with Kasumi and me.

"You know, he's my namesake," Kirk says, inserting himself into our conversation, but in a natural way, not an annoying one. "My parents named me after Captain Kirk."

"Really?" I say.

"Oh, yeah. Huge family of nerds," he says. Then he opens his mouth as if to say something else, but stops himself.

"That's why your mom had a badge for Angeles Comic Con," I say. "She's a nerdy girl."

He nods. Then I watch his eyes see something behind me and then he looks like he's going to say something again, but before he speaks, I feel someone grab my butt from behind and then throw their arms around my shoulders so I won't know who it is. I'm so surprised that I yelp and let go of the printed tickets left in my hands and they flutter to the ground. Then I elbow the person behind me.

"Ow," I hear Yuri say.

I turn around and find him doubled over from where I elbowed him in the gut and Phil and Tze laughing at him. I'm livid. When he uncurls himself to face me, I push him.

"What are you doing?" I yell. "You can't just grab a girl's butt from behind."

Phil starts laughing even harder.

"How could he resist?" he asks between guffaws. "I mean, look at that skirt. It's so *short*."

Kasumi hands me back all the tickets that fell to the ground.

"That's the way the costume was," I say. "That's the style from the sixties."

"You look hot," Yuri says, smiling big.

"It doesn't mean you can grab my butt," I say.

"Sorry!" Yuri says. He looks genuinely sorry and then he leans in and kind of whispers, "I always touch your butt when we're alone."

"That's when I know it's you," I say.

"You're right," Yuri says. "Can we start again?"

He looks at me sheepishly and I reluctantly let him kiss my cheek.

"What are you wearing?" I ask. He's wearing black pants and a Star Trek hoodie. He's *nerded* up but not *dressed* up.

"It's a Trek look," he says. "I'm cosplaying as the brand."

"Like DisneyBounding," Kirk says.

"Whatever that means," Yuri says.

"But this is a cosplay club," I say. "We all agreed that we'd come to the movie in cosplay."

Yuri shrugs.

"Next time it's not cool that you come," I say to Phil and Tze. "You quit the club. This is a club thing."

"I still like movies," Phil says.

"And I'm undecided about the club," Tze says. "I haven't committed either way."

"They're my friends," Yuri says. "I bought him and Tze tickets."

"With club money?"

"Don't be mad," he says. "They *were* in the club."

I look at Kasumi and Kirk, who shake their heads

I hand Yuri a ticket for him, Tze, and Phil.

"Hey," he says. "I need that cash. We gotta get snacks, right? And I gotta get paid back."

I dig into my bag and hand him the cash.

"Phil and Tze have to pay you for your tickets," I say.

"I think that's everyone," Kasumi says. "I took everyone's order, so now that the treasurer is finally here, he can buy all the popcorn and candy."

"Don't forget to keep the receipt," I say.

"If I'd known that we could bring a friend, I would have invited Sophie," Kasumi mutters as she presses the list of orders into Yuri's hand and we head inside. The four of us, Kasumi, Tze, Yuri, and I all buy and help carry the various items.

We go and hand them out and when I look at my ticket to find my seat, I realize that in the shuffle when I dropped the tickets, I didn't put me and Yuri next to each other.

"Hey, Phil and Joss, can I swap with you so that I can sit next to Yuri?" I ask, sweet as pie.

"No way," Phil says. "I like my seat. I'm not in the group anymore, so the rules don't apply to me."

"If I switch with you, then I'll be sitting next to my sister," Joss says. "I already told you, we're separate."

"I want to sit next to Yuri," I say, hoping he'll understand.

"Come on, Phil, move," Yuri says.

"Nope," he says.

Yuri shrugs and gives me a look, like he's tried and now he's given up.

"We made up the random rule for this very reason," Nadine says, leaning over to join the discussion. "That way, there would be no cliquing up. Clubs are for expanding your social circle, not reinforcing group think."

I can't disagree. I made the rule. I just wanted to bend the rule.

"Well, *you* got different tickets," I say to Joss.

"That's different," Connie says from her seat. "They're siblings."

I set my mouth to a line and scooch all the way down until I find my ticket. I'm next to Gwen and Kirk.

"Hey," Kirk says.

"Hey," I say.

"Look," Kirk jokes. "It's Kirk and Spock. It's like the original series on this end of the row."

"Yeah," I say. It's kind of funny, but I'm not in a laughing mood.

I look at Kirk. I can tell that he can tell that something is wrong with me. And he's trying to make me feel better. Only it's about the wrong thing.

"That was lame of Yuri to grab your butt," he says.

"Well, he's my boyfriend and if he wants to grab my butt, he can," I say.

"Fair enough," Kirk says, putting his hands up in surrender.

I steal a glance at him. Now I can tell he's unhappy. It's funny how misery gets spread around so easily.

"It's stupid Phil that gets him going," I say.

"If you say so," Kirk says. "My friends aren't like that."

"What about Juan in the library?" I counter.

"Ouch. You're right," he says. "I guess sometimes we're all like that."

"See," I snap.

I angrily adjust myself in my seat, but our body parts keep touching. Finally, we settle into positions where we are leaning away from each other.

The lights go down and the trailers start. And there on the screen in front of us is the real reason that I initiated this outing, the first official long trailer for *Team Tomorrow*.

The lights dim. The WC logo comes up. You can hear a pin drop. No one is breathing. I am not breathing.

The music starts; it swoops. The screen fades up on an image of Gargantua. I lose my mind. I start whistling and clapping. The trailer starts with Gargantua as a little girl—feeling small and weak and helpless, in a life full of chaos, and just as she's about to get slammed, she starts to grow. And grow and grow and grow. My heart stops.

I feel it. I understand. She is me. Her origin story could mirror mine. I feel as though I've been sliced by neutrinos on the moon.

Then the screen explodes with the other characters and there is one heart-stopping shot after another. It's so much to process, I already want to go to the lobby and watch it one million times on my phone to dissect it frame by frame.

It's clear that they've plucked things from my favorite Team Tomorrow run, Schism II. But I think that it's likely too esoteric for most fans. Which is why it makes sense that the team they picked were Green Guarder, Magnetic Pole, Lady Bird, Phase, Tri Star, Figment, and a new character called Doll.

I'm kind of weeping at the end of it.

The only person as excited about it as me in our group is Kirk. He turns to me, his eyes glistening. He's got tears in his eyes like I do. And for one second I forget that I'm pissed off at the whole world and that we've been holding our bodies away from each other.

"Holy crap," he says, turning to me in the dark. "That looks like it's going to be so good."

"I know!" I say, and then lean over, and I squeeze his arm because I'm excited. He smiles at me sheepishly and then turns his face back to the screen.

The main feature starts and I'm engrossed. Sometimes Kirk leans over to me and whispers something about the film, making a little comment or aside. Sometimes it's me who leans over to him and whispers something. My snacks are with Yuri, who I was supposed to be sharing with, but without it being weird, Kirk shares his candy and popcorn with me. Sometimes, when we lean toward each other, our shoulders touch.

Halfway through the movie, I am feeling a little cold, and Kirk says, "Are you cold?" and then, before I answer, he takes the sweatshirt that he smartly brought with him and lays it over my legs so that I am warm.

When the movie is done, while almost everyone else in the theater is leaving, we wait all the way through the credits until there is the post-titles stinger. It's a blooper on the *Enterprise* and it's worth staying for.

The lights come up and somehow the magic of being in a dark movie theater dissipates. We shuffle out of the cinema and head to the lobby. I am walking at pace with Kirk, who I can't stop talking to about the movie and the *Team Tomorrow* trailer.

"Who's in for food?" Yuri asks. "On the club."

Kasumi and I roll our eyes. I'm about to say something, but decide to let it slide because I'm too buzzy from the movie.

And then with a start I realize that I have to step away from my conversation with Kirk and I don't want to. But I do. I pull myself away from him and move over to stand next to Yuri. Weirdly, it feels as though I am breaking a connection, like I just flipped something off and I've gone silent.

"Burgers sound good," Kirk says. He's standing across from me. Our half-finished conversation hanging in the air. Just dangling there. Waiting to be picked up again. Yuri's hand is rubbing the back of my neck.

"Yeah," I say. "Burgers."

About half of us go to In-N-Out Burger. And half head back home to make curfews and stuff.

A stray thought enters my brain. Maybe I'll be seated next to Kirk again. Maybe I can follow up on that thing he said. Maybe

I can ask if he caught the Easter egg that I did. Maybe we can watch the trailer again on his phone.

But I'm arm in arm with Yuri now. And I get wrapped up in that because it's hard not to. Except every once in a while, when Kirk's eyes catch mine from all the way down the table.

And somehow, even though we are four tables apart, in my mind it's like Kirk and I are sitting next to each other and talking.

Six

asumi flashes her phone to me.

"Bad news," Kasumi says as we sort through racks at the Goodwill to find stuff for our costumes. I'm looking for a good wide midriff waist belt that I can paint gold and put a G on, and Kasumi is looking for tunic-y things to do Arya from *Game of Thrones*. There are weird things you have to think of when you make costumes. Like making sure you have proper undergarments. Like little booty shorts. Or that your tights are opaque enough. Or that your back looks as good as your front.

"What's the news?" I ask.

I glance at her phone while pulling through a box of belts. It's an email from the school. I never read those. They are always boring, like assembly has been canceled. Or we're shortened to a half day. Or there will be sandbags due to flash flooding. Whatever. The bell will ring. And the day will feel just as oppressive with or without me knowing these things.

But this time, as I scan it, I take the phone from her hand and I really read it.

MEMO: No costumes allowed for Halloween.

"Wait, what?" I say. I scan the email again.

Due to the wide range of faiths and the possibility of offending various groups . . . the potential for disturbing images . . . the use of prop weapons and masks which focus on violence and anonymity . . . the school board feels that in order to ensure the safety of all students . . . Halloween costumes will be forbidden.

Any student wearing a costume will be sent home, and a black mark will be put on their record.

"But that was going to be our big dress rehearsal before HeroQuest Con," I say. "That day is all about costumes."

"I know," Kasumi says. "This blows."

"I'll have to put a memo out," I say. I whip out my phone and text the group. Immediately a bunch of dislikes and frowny faces pop up.

"See," I say, holding up my phone. "Everyone thinks this policy is stupid. We should complain."

"They won't understand," Kasumi says. "They are the man and they are bringing us down."

"Since when are you all into talking about the man?" I ask.

"In English class we're reading this book and, well, Sophie. You know her. The costume girl. She's in a bunch of my classes and she made a good point about oppression and . . ."

"Oh, right," I say. "That girl who is always kicking us out. She's like the Time Stream, watching the clock all the time."

Kasumi presses her lips together and doesn't say anything.

There is something behind her eyes these days. I can't quite pinpoint it. But it's like she's keeping a secret. I recognize it because I am keeping one myself. Your eyes dodge other eyes. They look at the ground. You pull on your hair. You dig your nails into your arm and leave deep moon marks. You shove a piece of food into your mouth to avoid blurting things out.

We don't keep secrets from each other. But now we are both full of secrets. And now it's becoming clear to me that I can't even feel one hundred percent great with Kasumi, and that bums me out.

But there is another thing. A little thing that kind of pokes up. I feel a bit jealous of Sophie. They have classes together and Kasumi and I don't. Maybe I'm worried that she'll replace me. I pull another belt out and try it across my waist. It's big and gold and perfect for my costume, but finding it doesn't seem so fun all of a sudden.

I was really looking forward to coming to school as Gargantua on Halloween. It feels like this year every single fun thing is being stripped away one by one.

Worse than that, I've failed two tests in the last two weeks. I may not have been the best student in the world before, but I didn't suck at school as much as I do now. It's like I can't concentrate on anything. It's like nothing that any teacher says to me or anything I study sticks in my brain.

"Well, it means that we don't get to work out the kinks of our costumes for HeroQuest Con," I say. "Kind of a big deal."

"The costumes will be great!" she says. "Everyone looked great at Star Trek. We'll look great at the con as well."

"Well, mostly everyone looked great," I mumble, thinking about Yuri and his half-assed try.

I'm waiting for Kasumi to finish trying things on in the dressing room when Kirk texts me. I notice that it's a private text, not part of the SEW group thread.

Read your rant on the group wall. Don't worry about the stupid costume rule. We can just bound.

What? I text back.

Like they do at Disneyland. DisneyBounding.

He's said that phrase once before, but I don't know what it means.

I don't know what that is, I text.

The Disney parks won't let adults cosplay like the little kids, Kirk explains. *So people DisneyBound. They wear contemporary versions of their favorite characters. Basically, it's closet cosplay.*

It doesn't have to be Disney? I ask.

Of course not. Contemporary version of your fave character. I'll post it on the board.

Kasumi emerges from the dressing room wearing two layered shirts, brown and tan, and a pair of baggy brown pants.

"What do you think?" she asks.

I glance up from my phone and give her a thumbs-up.

"Ugh, I hate dressing rooms," she says when she's back in her street clothes and I'm still looking at my phone. "Are you and Yuri love texting?"

I shake my head.

I look back down at my phone. It's got those little dots . . . just blinking. I wonder if I should text something back. But now I think I've waited too long. The . . . stops blinking and I know that my little flurry with him is over.

TEAM TOMORROW

Various Gargantuas through the Years

Seven

A few days later, after carving pumpkins, I realize that lately, my grandmother is like a bear. She gathers herself to become as big and solid as she can as she lays down rules of the house. Trying desperately to keep us together. She uses lots of words like "You will do this!" "Because I say so." "I know what is best here."

She doesn't say it just to me. She says it to my mother as well. And it makes me angry and so I explode. I don't remember who started the screaming.

I just know that my grandmother and I are screaming so loudly that my mother comes out and screams. We are a house of screaming women.

Curses fly through the air like arrows in a medieval battle, landing everywhere and wreaking havoc. Hurts are targeted and old emotional wounds dug into for maximum pain. Things are said that just lay there for everyone to see. The monsters that crouch inside of all of us come out of boxes and cannot be put away.

We are three women in this house right now, with strong individual personalities. And everything is coming to a head.

My mother in her robes, her skin almost translucent from lack of sun, looking more like a ghost than a woman, trembles. She weeps and holds on to the chair in front of her to help her stand. She says things like "I can't. I just can't." "This can't be my life." "It's too hard."

"It's not," my grandmother screams. "This isn't who you were." "Snap out of it."

My mother and father always seemed like a unit. They had their places with each other. I knew they had met in the biz, at some Hollywood function when she was a high-powered executive. I know she decided to become a stay-at-home mom. She had an online vintage kids clothing business for a while. Ran the PTA at my elementary and middle school. Would laugh with her friends over wine about how she'd given it all up to be a domestic goddess because she could. Because my father could afford it. But it never struck me until now that she had given so many parts of herself away. She had bet on him, and now that it turned up short, she didn't know how to start from scratch.

It makes me so angry that she did that because it left her like this, incapable and weak.

Gargantua, when she turned against Team Tomorrow, fixated on her former team's weaknesses. She used them as the reasons she wouldn't be pulled back or tempted to rejoin them. She exploited them.

I am in my mask. But I am not hiding behind it. I am trying to take up as much space as I can so that I can be seen. So that they can try to see that I am being affected. That I should be able to weigh in. I say things like "You don't understand." "Stop telling me what to do here." "You've all ruined my life." "You are so pathetic." "I hate you."

It's the *I hate you* that turns the tide. You'd think it would be all the other things that flew around the room. But when I say, "I hate you both. I hate you all," they join together in turning on me. Something has united them at last.

"Don't ever say that," my mother says, shaking. "Not ever. Not once."

"Your problem is that you have it easy and you don't know it," Grandma Jackie says, and it's not clear who she's saying it to.

"I don't have it easy," both my mother and I scream at her.

"She's not talking to you, and yes, you do have it easy," my mother says. "My husband is sequestered."

"Then why don't you go back there?" Grandma Jackie says. "Go back to work."

"Yes," I say, now the alliances have shifted and I'm on a team. "Go back to work. Get out of the house."

"I've been out of the workforce for too long," Mom says.

"So you're blaming me for not having a career?" I say.

"He might have harmed old friends, so how could I possibly reach out to them for support? Or do anything to get myself back in the game and out of this mess?

"I'm a stay-at-home mom. I made my peace with it," my mother says, sounding defeated.

Grandma Jackie sounds hurt. "I thought I was setting an example for you, being a working mother. It wasn't easy in my day to get where I got. I took a bit of time off, a little longer than others, and that set me back, but I got back in there. What did you do? You threw your career away. I don't understand young women today. Why did I march?"

"You always make this about you," my mother says. "You don't understand what I do. It's about mixing and mingling. Networking. I'm out of the game."

"Well, you can't mix and mingle from the couch!" I yell. "I mean, when Gargantua left Team Tomorrow, she didn't crumble into a nothing. She started her own team. She went out and started again. Be like Gargantua!"

"You want me to start wearing a ridiculous mask and strut around in all of these costumes you keep trying to make, like you do?" my mother asks.

I am so angry. How dare she make fun of me when I am actually giving her good advice.

"How can you say that? Are you—" (And then I say a string of curses that I really regret.)

"Unacceptable," my grandma Jackie says. "Both of you are being unacceptable."

"I will think of how to punish you, Edan," my mom says.

"My life is punishment enough," I scream.

"GO. TO. YOUR. ROOM." They say it in unison; the alliances have changed again. Life really is like a comic book sometimes.

I take the first thing in front of me. A coffee mug. I fling it at the floor and it smashes into one million pieces.

I feel one hundred times better when it smashes, but I also feel one hundred times worse.

My mother points to my room without a word, but for a flash, she looks like she's got a fire inside her. I strut off. I feel strong and tall when I leave the kitchen, as if I did a good deed by making her get huffy. Then I shrink a little smaller when I reach the hallway, feeling like I am wearing the inside of me on the outside. When I enter my room, I collapse with guilt onto my bed and I am the size of a crying baby.

I don't know how long it is until Grandma Jackie comes in. Maybe ten minutes. Maybe a few hours. Time means nothing to me anymore. It folds quick and it stretches long.

Grandma Jackie doesn't knock, but I know better than to make a fuss out of it. She looms in the doorway.

"What am I going to do with you?" she says, sounding somewhat exasperated, and her voice thick with emotion.

"I don't know," I say. "I just hurt everywhere."

While I've been waiting, I've come up with a billion punishments for myself. All things that I think will be terrible.

"There are all kinds of ways to be a strong woman," she says. "And sometimes being strong looks like being weak."

"It's like everyone is talking but no one is saying anything," I say. "No one is listening."

"I'm listening," she says. "Starting next weekend, you will come to my pediatric ward in the hospital every few Saturdays until I say you are done, and you will visit with the children . . ."

I start to protest. She puts her hand up and gives me a look. A deathly look that, if it were an actual superpower, would probably kill me.

"You will come in costume," she says. "Every time a new costume. I will make you a list of the characters that the kids like the most. You will act like the character and you will be glad about it. You will cheer those children up."

"It's not fair," I say.

"Yes, you're right. It's not fair," my grandmother says. "But you are lucky. And you should know it. It's time to eat some humble pie and be thankful for all that you've got."

She shuts the door.

It's masterful of her, really, to put two things that I like, costumes and kids, together but to make it feel like a punishment. Forcing me to do it under her watchful eye is the punishment.

I flip my phone on and vague-post about it on our club board. I am hoping that someone will like it or heart it or give me spiritual hugs.

Instead, it's total silence.

Just when I need someone to see me, I'm the invisible girl.

Eight

Gargantua's main color scheme is purple and black with a silver G, so when I get ready on Halloween morning, I put on a pair of purple fishnets and a deep purple dress with black stripes. I put the thick waist belt that I found at Goodwill and spray-painted silver. I take a tiny piece of fabric and tie it to myself like a Victorian capelet and pin a tiny button of Gargantua on it alongside a small vintage pin of the letter G. I do my hair 1950s style with a big pomp in front and an undercurl, just like Gargantua wears her hair in the first run of Team Tomorrow.

I know that it will be annoying to wear high-heeled shoes to school, and we're not really allowed anything over two inches, so instead, I put on some Doc Marten boots that I always forget to wear. The purple doesn't quite match, but it's close enough and they are high enough to look like superhero boots.

I am dress-code compliant but also Gargantua-evident.

"What are you wearing?" Kasumi asks when I meet her in front of school.

"I'm bounding, like we said we would," I say.

"Did we say that?" she asks. "I don't remember."

"Kirk said it," I say. "On the group text, there was a thread."

"Oh," she says. "I guess I missed it."

But now that I think about it, I remember that he only texted it to me, off-list. On the group, we all just complained. I was the only one who mentioned it deep in the comments on the club board. And Kirk put a thumbs-up on that.

It's another thing that makes me feel off with her. In the old days I feel like she would have noticed a buried deep comment in a way too long comments thread.

"Are you mad at me?" she asks, looking genuinely concerned that I'm angry.

"No," I say. I'm just irritated that as we walk into school, I see that no one else from SEW has bounded except Kirk. He's all in green, and even though he looks like himself, he also somehow completely embodies Green Guarder. He's even wearing a green buttonier.

"You look great," he says when he sees me. "But can I just do something?"

"Sure," I say.

"Not here. We need pins," he says. "Follow me. We have time before first period."

"Oh, hey, go," Kasumi says to me. "There's Sophie, and I wanted to ask her about our homework before class, so . . ."

"OK, I'll see you later," I say.

I follow Kirk into the building and we go to the costume room, which is dark and empty.

He grabs my hand and his skin is warm, and I feel a little thrilled when he pulls me to the corner where our rack is, where the bags that hold our materials hang, along with capes and bodysuits and fur things. Kirk grabs some stuff out of one of the bags and spins me to face him.

"Lift," Kirk says.

I lift my hands over my head. Kirk takes the tape measure and slides it around my waist.

"Lower," he says.

I lower my arms. He takes some pins from a pincushion. He puts a few in his mouth to hold them. It makes his lips purse in a way that excites me. But also looks dangerous. He pulls at the fabric at my shoulders, and pins.

His face is near my cheek as he does it. I can feel his breath.

I swallow.

"Turn," he says.

I turn and he runs his hand down my back to smooth out the fabric. I feel a bit sad when his hand leaves just before it gets to the small of my back.

He gets to his knees and starts pinning the hem of the dress.

"Straighten," he says.

And I stop slumping and fix my posture.

He tugs at the skirt and nods to himself. Then he looks up at me from the floor.

"I think it's done," he says. Then he stands and guides me by my shoulders over to the mirror.

I swallow again.

Somehow, pinned and darted the way he did, it looks better than I could ever have made it. More *right*. There is something raw and beautiful about it. It's pinned together, not even sewn, and yet it looks beautiful. I look beautiful.

"How did you do that?" I ask. He knows more about sewing than I do. Than any of us do, I think. He's always reminding everyone how to use the machines.

He smiles.

"Sewing Made Simple," he says. "Didn't you read it?"

Kirk was the one who left the book for me at the library just when I needed it most. I must have read that book a hundred times this summer.

"I owe you one," I say, turning to him. Meaning for this fix, but also for putting the book in my path at the library this summer.

"You can pay me back by buying me French fries sometime," he says.

"Sure," I say.

"Great," he says. "It's a date."

"OK," I say.

But it's so curious that he doesn't say when. Like it doesn't matter. Like there is no hurry for French fries with me. And surely he just means as a friend. Because friends can get French fries. And we're just friends, because I have a boyfriend and it's not Kirk. Even though I probably feel prettier from the fix to my dress that Kirk did than from any of the one million times that Yuri has said I look hot.

The first bell rings and Kirk pulls his eyes away from mine and moves to put the sewing stuff away and heads out the door. But I do a little twirl by myself in front of the mirror.

He really helped.

Maybe when things are taken away, new things arrive.

Nine

I don't want to go home after school because I don't want to face up to Grandma Jackie and Mom after the weekend's explosion. I know that Grandma Jackie is on shift and won't be there. And that my mom will be in her room and won't notice. Still, I want to linger after school.

I see Kirk in the quad talking to Juan. He catches my eye and makes like he's going to move toward me. Like maybe he's going to say that now is the time to go for fries. Him as Green Guarder, me as Gargantua. But I spy Yuri coming down the stairs, and so I just give a short wave to Kirk and I catch up with Yuri, who is hanging out on the steps with Phil and Tze.

Yuri hugs me, but I can feel Phil glaring at me.

"What are you wearing?" he asks.

"I'm Gargantua," I say.

"Oh," Yuri says. "I see it now."

"Tell me, did you like this stuff before going out with Yuri? Or did you start liking it to get with Yuri?"

"I've liked Team Tomorrow since I was a little girl," I say.

"That doesn't make you a geek," Phil says. "There's, like, an epidemic of fake geek girls in this school."

"Like a zombie plague," Tze says.

"Fake geek girls?" I ask. "Are you Geek Gatekeeping? What does make me a geek? Is there some magical line?"

He saw me at Angeles Comic Con. He saw me playing video games at Yuri's house. He saw me talking excitedly after the Star Trek movie. He knows that I really like these things. I find that I am starting to go toward him to get in his face, but Yuri pulls me back and kind of pins my arms and laughs a little.

"I'm out of here," Phil says. "Have fun with your nerd girl."

Tze shrugs and jets off after Phil.

"What is his problem?" I ask. "Does he not know what a nerd is? I feel like he's playing me."

"It's just you have to admit that there are a lot of people who say that they are geeks who aren't really geeks," Yuri says.

"I don't see that," I say. "I see a lot of geeks geeking out about the stuff that they geek out about."

"Yeah, but they're not real geeks," Yuri says as he puts his arm around my shoulder and we start walking toward Vermont Avenue to get some coffee.

"Being a geek is being enthusiastic about things," I say, feeling a little bit irritated. "I see a lot of enthusiastic people."

"But it's more like they're jumping on a bandwagon," Yuri says. "You see that, right?"

"No," I say. "There's no entrance exam. If you say you're a geek, you are a geek. Why do you even hang out with Phil?"

"Phil's a really good guy," Yuri says.

"Except when he's a jerk," I say. "He really has a chip on his shoulder."

"Let's drop it," he says. "I don't think I'm saying things right."

"Yeah," I say. "I think maybe we're having a misunderstanding here."

"I don't want to fight," he says.

We're at the diner and we're sitting there and looking at each other and not doing homework.

He smiles. I smile. He smiles wider and touches my hand.

"I can't believe Halloween is almost done," he says. "That means it'll soon be, like, December already."

"Yeah," I say.

"What are you going to do for the winter break?" he asks. "Are you going away?"

"No," I say.

"We're going to Mammoth to ski," he says.

"That's cool," I say. "My family is doing something low-key."

And by low-key I mean we're doing nothing because we're still on hold about my dad going on trial.

Yuri runs his hands through his hair.

"What should I get you? Me and you somewhere alone?" he asks.

"That'd be nice," I say, excited that he's even thinking of getting me something.

"We don't get to be alone too much."

He's right. I never bring him to my house. And his house is always full of people. It's almost like no one in his family, including him, likes to be alone.

"Oh, hey," I say. "Before I forget, we need that SEW money for that bolt of black fabric."

"We don't have it," he says.

"Why not?"

"Things cost more then I thought," he says. "There were those other club expenses. Like the prints for the character portraits. It'll have to wait till the next month's dues."

"But I gave you all that cash," I say.

"Yeah, it just goes fast. I've got all these receipts people keep giving me."

"OK," I say. "We'll have to tell people that there is a cap on supplies and things. And we'll have to figure out black fabric for people to use. We promised, and don't forget that QuestHero Con is Thanksgiving weekend."

Yuri's face screws up. Then he starts packing his stuff away.

"Are we leaving?" I ask.

"Yeah," he says. "I gotta go."

But it's still early and he looks like something is irritating him. I can't imagine what it is. I worry that it is me and all my talk about fake geek girls not being a real thing.

But I can't just say nothing about that. He has to understand that it's stupid.

We walk in silence to his car. I want to say something but I don't. Because I'm afraid he'll snap or yell or break up with me.

It makes me feel weird to have to walk on eggshells. To be dictated by his mood. But lately, I can't tell which way is up. Just like when Magnetic Pole scrambled things. My own moods are so stormy that I can't blame someone else for being the same. So I just don't say anything.

He pulls up to my driveway and puts the car in park. He turns to me and he looks beautiful in the streetlight that streams through the car window.

He leans over and kisses me, and we kiss, soft and then a little more intensely.

"I'm sorry things got weird," he says.

I breathe a sigh of relief.

"Yeah," I say. "Let's not be weird."

"You're the tastiest," he says, and kisses me and nibbles on my neck, which makes me laugh. I slide my arms around his neck and pull him in close, resting my head on his shoulder.

"I'm a whole feast."

"Nerd," he says.

"Real nerd," I say.

"Yeah," he says. "Real nerd."

Any storm I thought was coming with Yuri passes.

TEAM TOMORROW

The thing that Gargantua didn't like about Team Tomorrow was how good it had to be all the time. But that is a lie. Every bad person is a little good. And every good person is a little bad.

The rest of the team said that she betrayed them by walking away and switching sides. That was the only way they could keep their hero narrative intact and delude themselves into thinking they were good and right.

Gargantua didn't see it like that.

Being a hero is *complicated*.

Gargantua didn't want to live a lie.

She believed that you don't compromise your ethics once you firm them up. Stick to your guns until you can't. And then you bail.

But that wasn't the reason she walked away from the team.

She walked away because she couldn't stand the duplicity of betrayal. How they wiped out her history. How she was alone in time. How they didn't admit that it made them less than good. That it made them the bad guys, too.

Gargantua could have stayed if they admitted that being a hero was emotionally messy.

After all, good is evil to evil and evil is good to good.

It just depends on how you look at the story.

Ten

I don't have time to make a million costumes, so I'm in a store-bought Wonder Woman outfit and Grandma Jackie hovers over me as I hand in the paperwork to start my first day at the hospital.

"You'll hang out in the playroom," she says as we both slather our hands with sanitizer. "I need you to wash your hands often."

She leads me down a hallway, and there is a full playroom at the end of the hall. Inside is a pool table and toys and video games.

A life assist coach nods at us as we enter the room. "Oh, great! You're here! I told the kids that a special visitor was coming. They'll be along soon."

There is a toddler with a big scar on his head, playing with some kind of hammering toy.

"What am I supposed to do?" I ask Grandma Jackie, suddenly nervous about everything.

"Just talk to the kids," she says. "Be in character."

"They're going to think it's lame," I say.

"No, they aren't," Grandma Jackie says. "They need it."

"Oooh! Wonder Woman," a teen says as they come in. He's bald and is rolling his IV. I snap and strike a heroic pose. It's interesting, because a Wonder Woman pose is different from a Gargantua pose. Heroes are mighty in different ways.

"I'll pick you up in two hours," Grandma Jackie says. "I've got things to do."

As she leaves, more kids come in. They are in all states of illness. Some have their IVs. Some wear face masks. Some are in wheelchairs. But when they see me, they all shout out, "Wonder Woman!" and smile.

The life assist coach fires up some superhero soundtrack music. I don't tell her that Marvel movies and DC movies are different. Heroic music is heroic, so I just go with it and I start to strike a lot of different poses, feeling out the Wonder Woman inside me. Some of the littler kids want to talk to me, thinking that I really am Wonder Woman, and they confess to me that they know my secret identity. The teens tell me their theories about the movies, books, and animated shows. Everyone passionately talks about their favorite DC characters. And I am glad that we can all relate to something together, even though it's not my thing.

Nerdy stuff really does bring people together.

And as far as my eyes can see, there are no fake nerds here in this playroom. Everyone is excited.

It gets a little boring posing, and after talking a while, the teens drift over to the pool table and video games and I'm left kind of doing nothing. So when I see a kid who doesn't care at all about me being there, but is at a table crafting, I get an idea.

"I know," I say. "Let's hand out paper and markers and draw our favorite superhero character."

"That's a great idea," the life assist coach says, and helps settle everyone in. The kids draw every kind of comic book character, from Team Tomorrow to the Justice League to the Avengers. There are even superheroes that I don't know. And some kids invent their own.

Before I know it, Grandma Jackie is in the room, tapping me and peering over my shoulder at the kids' drawings.

"I'm going to go back to the Invisible Jet now," I say out loud. There's a bit of protest.

"I'm sure we'll see her again soon," Grandma Jackie says.

"Yeah," I say. "But I might morph into someone else."

A lot of the kids hug me, or if they're not allowed, they blow me kisses, and that really surprises me.

"Looks like you were a hit," Grandma Jackie says as we head down to the garage.

"I am so ready to go," I say to her. "I'm wiped out."

"You did great," she says.

"Am I off the hook?" I ask.

"Nope," she says, patting me on the arm.

I am bone tired and quiet as I sit in the car, staring out the window on the drive home. It's too exhausting to do alone. I think to myself about all those vigilante characters and how hard it must be for them to do things alone all the time. No wonder Gargantua didn't last five issues by herself before she got herself some minions.

That's what I need. Minions. Well, not minions. But I'm going to need to recruit help if I'm going to make it through my next visit.

When I get home, I collapse on my bed, not even taking off my Wonder Woman costume and boots, and write out a post to the SEW group before I fall deep asleep.

EMERGENCY: *Help needed. Recruiting team members:*

I start a thread asking for help.

I clearly outline all the steps needed to apply. I link to the form at the hospital.

But somewhere, before I nod off, I realize that as tired as I am, too tired even to eat, I feel a little full inside.

Eleven

Because there is no black fabric for everyone to use, I get the idea that everyone should bring in any old black clothes to SEW meeting for us to dismantle and distribute to whoever might need it. We got a few bagfuls. I'm glad for the fabric because now I have to do a few extra costumes per my grandma's list, and I can't buy them all. I want to make some of them. It will make it more fun for me.

"Who can stay an hour more today and give a few hours in the coming days to break this stuff down so we can hand it out?" I ask.

Pretty much no one raises their hands except Kasumi, Kirk, Joss, and Gwen.

"I can do some time in the next few days," Scott says.

"Me, too," Nadine says. "I have to be home to help with my baby brother today."

"Yuri?" I ask.

"Sorry," Yuri says. "I've got things to do after school this week. History project."

That is the trouble with clubs. Everyone wants to be in one, but they want all the benefits without doing any of the grunt work.

"We'll be fine," Kasumi says. "It'll get done."

"OK," I say. "Thanks, all. And pay your dues!"

I thought we had more in the coffers. I'd collected the cash and gave it to Yuri, but when I looked, Yuri was right, the club account was pretty low.

As people leave, a few stuff some cash into the bowl I set out. Others whip out their phones and I can hear the ping of notifications on my smartphone as people PayPal me money to our club account.

Then it's just me, Kasumi, Joss, Gwen, and Kirk.

"Well," I say, handing each one of them a bag. "Let's get to it."

We each take a station at the big sewing table and unbag the donated clothes. After working in silence for a while, we start talking.

"What should we do with the non-black pieces of fabric?" Kasumi asks, holding up a piece of bright pink lining she tore out from a skirt.

"Throw it out, I guess?" I say.

"No," Kirk says. "We should hold on to it all. Someone might need it."

Kasumi looks at the pink and then nods.

"Yeah," she says. "I could use this for my Izabel costume from Saga. That's what I want to try next."

I pull a piece of houndstooth out of the garbage underneath my station.

"I guess this could work as a back piece for Gargantua," I say.

We work in silence again, until Kirk starts talking.

"How did you become such a big Team Tomorrow fan?" Kirk asks me as he unstitches a black dress.

"I can trace my love for Team Tomorrow to watching the cartoon," I say. "I watched it, loved it, and then when I was about nine, I saw an omnibus in a comic book store window. I begged to go in and get it. And I was hooked."

Kirk nods as he brings the fabric up to his mouth and pulls at something with his teeth. I don't know why he doesn't use the scissors. But also, I like that he looks kind of feral when he does it.

"The comic books are better than the cartoon," I say. "They go deeper. They flow better."

"I started with the comic books," Kirk says. "My dad left when I was little. But he left a bunch of his stuff behind. When I was about nine, my mom and grandma needed space for a business they were starting, so I had to go out and clean the garage."

"We both discovered it at nine," I say.

Somehow that warms my heart. The thought of two little kids falling in love with something at the same time but not being able to share that love until years later.

TEAM TOMORROW

Lady Bird was introduced when Gargantua went rogue. She was the perfect match for Green Guarder. He was green and made things bloom. She was like a hummingbird. All brilliant colors and comfortable in a garden. Lady Bird was a little person who was half woman and half bird. She flies and has a shrieking cry. Her hands can turn into talons that inflict a lot of damage during melee.

Gargantua had it out for Lady Bird.

In every battle she waged against Team Tomorrow, she concentrated her efforts on Lady Bird. It was pure jealousy. A fiery rage.

Green Guarder could never understand it. In the penultimate story arc, issues 54–62, Lady Bird, her wings broken, looked up at Green Guarder, who held her in his arms and wept.

"Don't you understand?" Lady Bird cooed. "She loves you."

"She does nothing but destroy," Green Guarder said.

"And you make things bloom," Lady Bird said. "You're a perfect match."

Then Lady Bird died.

And when I say died, I mean that by issue 81, she was alive again. In comics that's the way things happen. You die. You live. You are reborn. You are bizarro. You are a parallel you. You are a clone. You are rebooted.

But it was some damn fine comics.

And even though I didn't want Gargantua to rejoin Team Tomorrow and I liked her being rogue and on her own, I couldn't help but cry.

Comics can make you cry.

They can shove their mighty fist into your chest and rip out your heart.

Twelve

When the next Saturday that I have to volunteer rolls around, I make my way to the hospital on the bus. It takes forever. The bus drops me right in front of the children's hospital. I am not ready to go in yet, so I cross the street to the Starbucks to get a coffee.

I am zoning out standing in line, when I notice someone by the sugar counter. It's Kirk. He's preparing two coffees.

"Hey," I say, poking him in the back. "You made it! Thank you!"

He turns around and looks at me blankly. He looks like a little boy, holding the two cups of coffee in his hands as though they are going to keep him standing up.

"What?" he asks.

I ramble on about the thing that I am doing. Visiting the kids. Prattling about being in trouble. Talking a mile a minute and not taking a breath. I'm almost giddy.

"I'm so happy that I don't have to do this alone," I say. "It was really nice of you to show up."

He looks at me again. Kind of stutters. Then sets his face to a determined and relieved look.

"My costume is in my car," he says.

"Oh," I say. "OK. Meet you in there?"

"What floor again?" he asks.

"Third floor. Meet me at the nurses' station?"

"Give me half an hour?" he says.

"Sure," I say. "I'm not really ready to go in there. Today it's going into rooms instead of the playroom."

"Then I'll meet you here. We'll go together," he says. "I hate going into hospitals alone, too."

I point to a table and he nods and then exits the door.

It's only hours later that I wonder where he was going for thirty minutes and why he had two coffees in hand.

"This is my grandma Jackie," I say, introducing Kirk to her when we get to the ward.

"Thank you for coming," she says. Then she gives me a look, like this was supposed to be a solo thing. But then another look that says, *I get that you didn't want to come alone, and I'm going to let it slide because you are still doing the thing.*

"The children will be very happy to have two superheroes visiting them." Then she reviews with us some health and safety instructions and leads us to the double doors.

We both go into the bathroom to change from boring old us to Team Tomorrow. I've really pulled together my Gargantua, wanting to try it out for HeroQuest Con coming up. I've adjusted some pieces, and hand sewn in some triangles to give my costume texture. The houndstooth kind of gives the impression, when I walk, of how Gargantua grows in the animated show. They use a pattern like that in the cartoon as an effect. I even bought a special pair of short shorts that kind of smooth everything out.

Kirk emerges and it's the first time I've seen him in full Green Guarder. It kind of makes me stop, because he looks so much like him. Except his hair is a little too short, but that's a minor detail.

"Wow," I say. "We look great."

But I mean that he looks great.

"Ready to fight the Time Stream, my liege," he says.

I admit that I kind of blush at the thought of him being one of my minions.

The life assist coach explains to us that we're going to be doing bed visits today. She gives us a list of rooms and opens the first door. I lead the way and Kirk follows, as it should be if we're going to go by the character canon. After all, Green Guarder always followed Gargantua around like a puppy.

I push open the swinging door and hold it for him as he walks through. The kids start screaming with delight. Kirk looks back over his shoulder to me and smiles. Grandma Jackie nods at me and goes on her way.

I go to the first bed and start talking to the girl.

There is solace in a smile. In knowing that you made someone who was in pain happy. It's almost like my emotional pain starts to disappear a little into the joy that swallows it.

I don't talk to Kirk the whole time we are there, going from room to room with our escort. It's just me and those kids and those smiles and him doing his thing. We are together and bound, as though we are a team but we are also individual, each doing our thing with our own skill. He makes the kids laugh out loud. I make them smile and confide in me. I like that.

After two hours, another nurse comes in and tells us it's time to go. The kids need to rest.

"So you'll come again in two weeks," Grandma Jackie says when we pass the nurses' station. She's there checking some charts. "There are always new kids in other wards and the play-room. And I think they'd like to see some Star Wars."

Grandma nods. And I know that it is her way of saying, *I'm sorry, but you're still on warning.*

"Just let me know when to be here," Kirk asks. "I do a good Kylo Ren."

I look at him. He's not even joking. My grandma looks from me to him and then back to me.

"We made a good team back there," Kirk says.

"Gargantua isn't really on the team anymore," I say. "She works alone."

"She used to be on a team," he says. "She could learn to be on one again."

I want to say that I felt connected. And I wonder if that's why Gargantua kept coming back even when she'd turned from her former teammates. A string from her to them that pulled her back. Even now, Kirk standing on the other side of the hallway, looking at me from under his bangs as if we have a secret together, is confusing.

His phone beeps and he looks at it and then curses. "I'll see you later." Then he runs and grabs an elevator, looking like a flash of green.

"So who's your friend?" my grandma asks.

"A guy from school," I say. "He's in my cosplay club."

"That was nice of him to help you," she says. "That was nice of you to let him help."

"I . . ."

I don't know what to say because if I say anything, it would be a lie. So I just stay quiet.

"Give me fifteen minutes to finish up here and I'll drive us home," she says.

I sink onto the bench in the hallway. I feel light somehow. The joy of the kids still sticking with me. But it's also something else. Like somehow Kirk left but I still feel as though I'm still attached to him. Like there is a string stretching from him to me.

My phone beeps and I check it.

It's Kirk.

Sorry I had to jet. Thx for letting me help with the kids. It did me a world of good.

I don't respond to Kirk.

But I have to admit that it did me a world of good as well.

Thirteen

When SEW leaves the school building in the two minivans that we ride-share to HeroQuest Con, we look good.

Here's how SEW breaks down for our outing to the con.

STAR WARS: *One Rey. One Kylo Ren.*
GUARDIANS OF THE GALAXY: *One Gamora. One Groot.*
GAME OF THRONES: *One Arya. One Jon Snow.*
TEAM TOMORROW: *One Gargantua. One Green Guarder.*
AVENGERS: *One Hulk. One Peggy Carter.*
DC COMICS: *Batgirl of Burnside and Harley Quinn.*

"Oh," I say, looking around at all the costumes. The minivan driver looks at us like we're a bit nuts. But also like he thinks it is a bit cool. He makes a big deal of telling us that Thor is his favorite character.

"Wow," Kasumi says, and squeezes my arm as we approach the hotel. HeroQuest Con is not as big at Angeles Comic Con, but it's still pretty impressive as we roll up and see all the costumed attendees.

When we get there, Kirk seems anxious. He keeps checking his phone as it keeps pinging. We're all in the lobby, looking at the program and taking it all in and making our plans.

"Hey," Kirk says. "I'm going to bail. I'll catch up with you all later, OK?"

"Sure," I say.

Even though a little weird part of me is bummed that I won't be spending some time with Kirk, which I was looking forward to, I remind myself that we're not all beholden to one another. Everyone wants to do a different thing. Some want to go to panels, some want to walk the floor. So we all split up.

"Whoever is going to do the costume contest, meet at the ballroom at 4:00 p.m. for check-in and prejudging," I say. There are only a few of us who entered. "Then everyone else, please come and cheer us on for the cosplay contest tomorrow."

Kirk nods and then dashes through the door to the exhibit hall.

"I wonder where he wanted to get to so fast?" Kasumi asks.

"I think they have toy exclusives and stuff," I say. "You know if you don't get it early, you miss out."

"I mean that is cool, but also, whatever, you know?" Yuri says. "They are just *toys*."

"Maybe he's a collector," I say.

"Yeah," Kasumi says. "Collectors are really serious about that kind of stuff."

"Well, good," Yuri says. "I didn't want to hang out with that guy."

They tolerate each other and play nice during club time, but I notice that Yuri and Kirk don't really interact with each other. It doesn't bother me, because we all have people we gravitate to and people we don't. But it's something that I am really aware of. How they both stand away from each other but close to me.

Yuri starts looking at the app map to figure out a game plan and then mumbles something about hooking up with Phil and Tze later. I roll my eyes, but it's not unexpected.

Kasumi, Yuri, and I want to start on one side of the floor.

"Let's start over by all the television stuff," Yuri says, having come up with a plan.

"What about clothes stuff?" Kasumi asks.

"We'll get there," Yuri says.

"What do you want to do, Edan?" Kasumi asks.

My eyes can't help but linger on the door where Kirk disappeared. What was it that called to him so in there? I want to know what it is. I want to see it.

I don't want to turn right when Kirk has turned right, because I don't want to admit that is where I want to go. That I want to talk to him about what we should go as next weekend at the hospital. I want to ask him if I should try Rey or Leia. That I wonder if I should ask him if we should meet for breakfast first. Or maybe French fries after. That maybe we could take a bus or a ride-share together. That I am happy to be here with Yuri and Kasumi, but there is a part of me that wants to spend time with him. And that makes me feel a bit weird and guilty. So to make up for it, I grab Yuri's hand and lace my fingers with his.

And I remind myself that whenever Gargantua felt a pull, she went the other way. I will follow suit.

"Let's start in aisle one hundred and go lane by lane," I say. Aisle 100 is the completely opposite direction of where Kirk went.

"That's Artist Alley," Kasumi says. "Cool."

Yuri reluctantly agrees to come with us to artist alley first, but we promise we'll check out the TV stuff right afterward.

By the middle of the exhibit hall floor, my feet are already killing me. High-heeled boots make me look taller, but it's no easy feat to walk in them. I push through the pain and the growing blister. The floor is packed with people and it's so full that it's hard to walk, even without the boots. People just stand in the middle of aisles. They have big bags on their backs. They go too slow or walk too fast. There are parts where the aisles are clear and wide, and others where we are packed into the con like sardines.

We finally get down to the end where there is artist alley and small press and cute clothes. And once again, I start wanting everything and am getting angrier by the booth that I can't afford anything. Kasumi buys a few things. Yuri keeps whipping out his card and getting things. I only take the free cards or swag and pictures of the things that I want to search for later.

"Hey, Kirk is over there," Kasumi says. "KIRK!" she yells.

My eyes follow over to where she is pointing. He's sort of standing by a rack of clothing inside a booth on the end of the aisle.

Kasumi waves her hands over her head as she calls his name again. His eyes catch us and then he disappears behind a rack.

"Let's go find him," she says. "Maybe he wants to eat lunch with us."

She pulls me along and Yuri follows us, but when we get to the booth, Kirk's gone.

"I wonder where he went," Kasumi muses, looking around.

"Who cares?" Yuri says. "Let's go to the food trucks. I'm starving for a burrito."

"Wait," I say. And I start to flip through the rack of clothes. It's vintage clothing, sweaters, dresses, shirts, skirts, but altered and made to be discreet geek chic. I've seen stuff like that before, but it always looks clunky. But these pieces are beautiful. They range in price from super affordable to very high-priced. I stand for a second in awe of a mannequin that is wearing a beautiful black 1950s cocktail dress with tiny appliqués of Team Tomorrow. It is something extraordinary and wonderful.

"That one is not for sale," the woman says. "It's an example of a commission dress."

She's rocking a Rosie the Riveter–like kerchief and she's wearing cool cat-eyes glasses. She's got on a sweater that's tastefully stitched with Star Trek fabric and a full poodle skirt that has the Star Trek emblem.

"I couldn't afford it anyway," I say.

Being in this booth, with these clothes that I love, feels as though I've stepped through a magic door. And like this old woman is a witch in the woods. But the kind that helps you become a princess. I could be a princess in that dress. A beautiful, gargantuan princess who could take on anything.

"I think that would fit you," the woman in the booth says. "You should try it on even though it's not for sale."

I shouldn't try it on, because I am wearing my Gargantua costume. But before I can say no, she pulls it off the rack. I go up to the long mirror and hold it up against me.

"It would really suit you," the old woman says. "You could wear it to a dance."

"How much is something like this?" I ask.

"Three hundred dollars," she says.

I shake my head.

"I couldn't even if I wanted to," I say.

She nods. But not in a way that is mean or makes me feel bad.

"One day," she says, "a dress like that will be yours."

I put the dress back up on the rack and step out of the booth.

It's like I went to Wonderland for a moment. And now, Yuri and Kasumi are staring at me and asking me if I want tacos, grilled cheese, or Asian fusion.

We head to the food trucks, but I can't stop thinking about that dress.

fourteen

Yesterday, I thought we looked good when we got to the con. I thought we looked good when we stopped and did photo ops at the various photo op spots on the floor. I thought we did well in the cosplay contest prejudging. But I quickly learn that there is this thing that can happen sometimes where you think you look really good. And maybe you do in one place but you certainly do not in another. Because today, when we all go backstage to wait for our categories to be called and to go onstage for the costume parade, I realize that we all look terrible.

Suddenly, I see our uneven stitches. The flimsy cheap fabrics. The not quite right accessories.

Sure, we look better than average. Better than someone on Halloween. Better than a lot of people on the floor who are just dressed up for fun. But compared to some of the craft and skill in this back room, I feel embarrassed.

"Please sort yourself into your fandom and character in your particular group," one of the costume organizers says.

We are all being separated into the category we entered in. I entered in Villains. Kirk entered in Heroes. There is also a Sidekick category. I have a little N on my number indicating that I am a novice. Other people have other letters to symbolize their level of cosplay mastery. You're judged by your level. That way, novices don't have to go up against masters.

I make my way over to stand with a bunch of other Gargantuas and other Villains and I feel small.

"Nice costume," an older lady who must be in her thirties says to me.

"I don't look that good," I say and indicated one of the other Gargantuas.

"First time?" she asks, noticing my N.

I nod.

"Pretty good for a first time," she says. "You'll get better."

"I just wanted it to be great," I say.

It feels like winning that walk-on role is the most important thing that I could ever want. It's the only thing that matters. And I know with a pure certainty that unless I learn how to become a master seamstress, I'm going to lose.

"Didn't you come in with him? He looks good," she says, and points to the line of heroes. He's standing with two other Green Guarders. There aren't that many of them, since there are other, better members of Team Tomorrow to cosplay. I realize that she's pointing at Kirk. And while I stand here, apart from him, just looking at him, I have to admit that he does look good.

"Yeah, I know him," I say.

"You could ask him to help you," another woman says.

"Villains, get ready, you're up next!" the organizer calls out. We all get into a line and walk over to the side of the stage. I glance back at Kirk, who I find is looking at me. He gives me a little wave and then a thumbs-up.

I'm nervous, I mouth.

Don't be, he mouths back.

I don't know if it's nerves because of going onstage or because I realize that Kirk was *looking* at me. Like I think I caught him checking me out. But then I think I must have made that up.

"Just go out there when they call your number, and have fun. Strut your stuff. Be tall and *Gargantuan*," the first lady says.

"Cosplay isn't all about the costume. It's about inhabiting the character," the other lady says. "Trust me. I'm a professional."

"Besides, you made it through round one of judging or you wouldn't be here," the first lady says.

"Is that what prejudging check-in was?" I ask. "I wondered why a few of us didn't make the cut."

They both nod. That makes me feel better. Like I already kind of won something.

The music comes on. They are playing the soundtrack, the one that's been released for the upcoming film. I know it's called "Today's Tomorrow Theme."

I hear my name and number and I head out onto the stage. It's like going from dark to light. It's like being born. The spotlight follows me as I move and lift my cape. I make three poses. The crowd cheers.

In the end, I don't get first or second or third place. I don't even make it into the top ten finalists. But I do get a certificate for embodiment of character.

When we rejoin the crowd, our friends surround us, clapping and whistling.

"Let me see," Kirk says when I meet everyone outside after picking up the certificate.

"It's like a participation award," Yuri says.

"They didn't give it to everyone," I say.

"'Cause I didn't participate," he says.

"I didn't get one," Kirk says. "I participated."

"I think you should have placed, Kirk," I say. "All the Gargantuas thought you looked great."

Kirk smiles.

"I did look great," he laughs. "But you can only win hero category if you're doing a more popular character, I think. And that Black Panther guy, a novice, was really way better than me."

"It was a good first showing," Kasumi says. "You looked so great."

"Now that I see how it's done, I think I'm going to enter next time," the Ferrar twins say at the same time.

I change into my sneakers so I can walk more.

"Should we go home?" Yuri whispers to me.

"No," I say. "There is more to see."

But the bell rings and an announcer comes on the PA, shutting down the con for the night.

I don't want it to be over. As long as I'm here, I'm her and not me.

And I like being her.

TEAM TOMORROW

Secret identities.

Not every superhero has a secret identity. The use of a secret identity is up to the hero. But many do. It's a way to protect the superheroes from villains. To protect their families from being used against them. To protect their ability to do their superhero work.

Some, in their civilian life, wear glasses or don a different hairdo. Somehow they are hidden in plain sight. Others are themselves while they are in their civilian guise and wear a mask while they are superhero-ing.

Gargantua was a lab technician named Greer Gorman. She was the brilliant assistant to a man named Dirk Wharton. Dirk, a cutting-edge infrared scientist, was the head of a lab at the Moon University. Greer was his gal Friday and his on-again, off-again squeeze. She did all of the actual practical work and research while Dirk published the papers and got all the credit.

In Gargantua's origin story, she has an experiment running, and Dirk Wharton meddles with her numbers, trying to squeeze a little more out of the experiment. This causes the lab to explode and the overcharged neutrinos to embed in her DNA and it caused her ability to grow and shrink, depending on her state of mind.

Dirk Wharton was killed in the accident.

Jeanne Bernier felt that his death was necessary so that Gargantua could become a wholly actualized hero.

There is a touching scene in the backstory issue of Team Tomorrow that explores all the characters' origins, where Greer Gorman is at Dirk Wharton's funeral. She starts off grieving for Dirk and in the first panel she is quite small, compressed by the grief. But throughout the funeral, other women who were his former assistants and girlfriends come to pay their respects and it becomes clear what a misogynist Dirk Wharton really was. Greer begins to grow bigger in each panel, until at the end, she is so large that she busts out of it. The panel actually cracks open and her body spills into the gutter. The final panel on the page shows her walking away, as tall as the trees in the cemetery.

It is never stated that Greer Gorman goes back to school to get her own PhD, but it is implied, for the Greer Gorman we know is not a lab technician or assistant, but a woman who has equal standing with the other scientists in a lab that works on rays of all kinds. We can infer that her secret identity keeps her safe and able to research her own condition, while also subtly telling the reader that women are capable and equal. This was stunning for the time when Team Tomorrow began, as women scientists were very rare. Most other female superheroes of the time were hidden behind the acceptable trades for women: Secretary. Nurse. Stewardess. Wife.

But regardless of profession, the dual life of the superhero is inherently fascinating for the very fact that at all times our heroes' lives are split. It interestingly mirrors the fact that every human is a bit different with each person and that, in fact, we hold many identities within ourselves.

fifteen

"Why are you still wearing your costume?" Yuri asks when he picks me up for the third day of the convention. "The costume parade was yesterday."

"Because we're going to a comic book convention," I say as though that should explain it all.

"Right," he says.

Almost no one else from our crew is wearing their costumes today.

It's only me, Nadine, Joss Ferrar, and Kirk who are cosplaying.

Even though today we all make our way to the convention center separately because for some weird reason we ended up having only enough club money for the ride-share together for one day, it makes me feel calmer when we hook up with everyone.

Today at the con, having already mapped the lay of the land the past two days, we are like a blob. First walking with some, then falling back to talk with others. There is a point after fish tacos where I don't want to hear the chitter-chatter of everyone. The ceilings are too high. My mask is bugging me. My feet still hurt. I want to hit a panel, Cosplay 101, so I can learn new things, but everyone wants to walk the floor some more and suddenly I want to break off from them, but it's hard to find a reason or excuse. These kinds of things are about compromise. Sort of do what the herd is doing.

That's not what Gargantua would do. She wouldn't just nod and say, *OK, let's go to the toy section for the billionth time.* She'd clearly state what she wanted to do. And she'd break off from the team.

So I do. I just let them all keep walking and I stop, and then they are gone. I am swallowed by the crowd behind them and I am left blissfully alone.

There is a corner I hadn't seen at the con where there are a bunch of creators and old actors tabling. People like pilot number two or green lady alien from that sci-fi show you liked! Voice actors from that video game you play! Illustrator of that one thing that everyone was obsessed with in 1972! It's a strange alley, with a disconnect between the pictures they have lying on the table to autograph at twenty bucks a pop and the now much older people standing behind the table, eagerly trying to draw you in.

I'm amazed at how crowded their tables are for the most part. They are doing a business and there is something cool, like they had touched some incredible part of fandom and it has stuck with them forever, and something sad, like they are stuck in time. Just as I'm thinking of that, I see her. It's a very old white-haired woman, perfectly coiffed, sitting daintly under a large image of Gargantua. Her name is in big gold letters above the very-old-school character image. JEANNE BERNIER.

I stop. She was one of the creators of Team Tomorrow. I check the name again. It's really her. No one is at her table. She's utterly alone and I wonder how that is possible when she is so famous. I'm standing in the middle of the aisle, staring at her as people push past me, going from here to there. And then our eyes catch. The old woman smiles at me, and claps her hands in a little applause. I unstick myself from where I am and walk to her.

"Your costume is lovely," she says with a slight French accent.

"Are you really Jeanne Bernier?" I ask.

She nods.

"I'm such a big fan," I say.

She smiles.

"What are you doing here?" I ask.

"I was asked to be a guest because of the movie, I think," she says. "But mostly, people only care about Hal. But since he's passed, they asked me."

"Are you going to be on a panel?" I ask. I want to make sure to note the time so I can go.

"No," she says. "I'm just here with my souvenirs."

I look down at the table and I realize that it's covered with rare Team Tomorrow memorabilia.

"You can touch them," she says, and I know immediately that she's placing great trust in me. I pick up the old issues, an original ashcan, a Gargantua doll, a breakfast cereal insert.

"Can I ask you something?"

"Go ahead," she says.

"Why didn't you create any other superheroes after Team Tomorrow?"

She sighs heavily. She looks down at her hands. Then she looks up at me.

"Have you ever been in love?" she asks.

I think about it for a second. I wonder if I'm in love right now. Part of me feels something bigger than I've ever felt, but I don't know if it's shaped the way it's supposed to be.

"Well, one day you will be," she says. "I was in love with Hal, and we created a world together. But in the end, the times were against me. He was a man and I was a woman and that was the end of things when our world broke."

"That sounds terrible and unfair," I say.

"It's different now, a little bit," she says. "But my one piece of advice to you is this: Always keep yourself intact even when you find your team. And never let a man hold all the power over your destiny."

When she looks at me, I think she knows me. My thoughts drift to my dad and the way Mom is crumbling. I think about how sometimes I bite the inside of my cheek to stay quiet when I'm with Yuri.

"I have to go," I say. "I have to meet my friends."

"Do you want me to sign something?" she asks.

"I don't have the twenty dollars," I say.

She takes a Sharpie and pulls out a Gargantua paper doll set from the 1970s from under her table and signs it.

"Here," she says, pushing it toward me. "I have a lot of these, and I think you are meant to have one."

"Oh, thank you!" I say. Then she looks past my shoulder and smiles at someone else. A small crowd has gathered and she starts to charm others.

I walk away like I'm walking on air. As though my time stream has been touched somehow with a powerful meaning that I can't quite parse yet.

I'm lost in my own thoughts, marveling at my luck when someone stops me.

"Can I take your picture?" a man says to me.

I stop and make a pose to take the picture. The guy puts his phone up, but then puts it down.

"You should smile," the guy says.

I don't feel like smiling, but I kind of do it anyway.

"Nice. And stand sexy."

"What?" I ask, my smile now gone from my face.

"You're a pretty girl," he says. "You should smile."

Instead of smiling, now I scowl.

"That's not very nice," he says. "Be nice. Do another one."

It's as though he's chastising me for being the Gargantua I

want to be and not the one that he wants. He moves toward me, his arms reaching for my waist, like he's going to pull me forward. I see his arms coming for me and my instinct is to slap him away, but also I don't want to be a mean person, and then these two thoughts in my head crash into each other and I'm frozen and the strange guy is touching me.

"Whoa!" I say. "Hands off."

Suddenly, Kirk is in front of me.

"What's going on here?" Kirk asks the dude.

I stand behind him now that he's here so that he's blocking my body from view from the camera guy.

"Why don't I take a picture of both of you," the guy says. "Green Guarder and Gargantua."

"Nah," I say. I peek over from behind him and see that the guy is pissed. "Cosplay is not consent."

"Why don't you move along," Kirk says to the dude and he's got his arms out, one of them on the shoulder of the guy, pushing him away from me.

The guy curses, says something about girls at cons being big teases, and then moves along.

"You OK?" Kirk asks.

I am glad he was there, but somehow instead of thankful, which I should be because it's Thanksgiving weekend, things come out hard and angry, sounding the way Gargantua would to Green Guarder.

"You don't have to protect me," I say.

"I have this under control," I say.

"I am a self-rescuing princess," I say.

"You think I don't know that?" Kirk says to me. "But sometimes even self-rescuing princesses need help."

I notice that he kind of sounds like an antihero when he says it, which makes a smile almost flutter up. But I stop it in its tracks and get tough with him.

"Well, I don't," I snap. Why do I snap when I don't mean to? I feel so coiled up inside that prickliness just springs out of me sometimes.

He takes a step back, as though I've pushed him with an invisible force. Then he shakes his head in disbelief and moves away from me, like he was never in front of me.

And I feel funny.

I move along, trying to process what I'm feeling. I'm mad at that photo guy. Mad at myself. Mad at Kirk. Mad at the world.

When I get to the WC booth, I remember that there is a Team Tomorrow photo op. You can pose in front of a panel from one of the comics and they have thought balloons that you can put over your head. "My Liege!" "Kapow!" "Onward and to Tomorrow!" "This is doom!" "Time to be a hero!" They have the logo of the film on top when they print it out. I got myself a photo yesterday, but I want another one. I notice that Kirk is in the WC booth as well. He's standing in a line waiting for his turn to talk to the current artist of Team Tomorrow.

"Hey," I say, coming up to Kirk, awkwardly trying to make up for being mean before. It is easier to muster up confidence when I am Gargantua. "Green Guarder. Come forth."

Kirk looks up from the line that he's standing in. He's now getting a sketch done by the artist. He looks busy. And like I'm irritating him. I try not to let it bother me.

I point to the photo line and smile. And then I go stand in it. I don't wait to see if he's coming. I just go. He doesn't come for a while, and I think, *Crap. He's not going to join me.*

Then I think, *Crap. Why do I even care?*

I'm still alone in the line when it's my turn and thinking that it doesn't matter. I abandoned the group because I wanted to be alone. This is where and how I want to be. I am going to own it. I imagine myself, the hero of the moment, forging my own way, when the photographer interrupts my flight of fancy and asks, "Back for seconds?"

"I guess so," I say as I step in front of the green screen.

"Wait. We're together," I hear, and suddenly Kirk is there. "My liege."

Kirk does a little flourish to me and all that irritation that we both had is gone.

"Great," the guy says. "How do you want to do this?"

Kirk and I look at each other. Then look at the photographer.

"Can we do two?" we both say in unison.

"Sure," he says.

Without talking about it, we do one where we are in each other's faces, fighting like we are enemies. Just like the arc where they are on opposite sides of the Time War, when Gargantua believed in yesterday and Green Guarder believed in today. They both thought it was the only way to tomorrow.

They were both right and wrong.

And acting it out, it feels good to do that, like really we're getting something out of the way. Although I don't know what. I don't dislike him at all.

Then Kirk moves behind me and slides his arms around me in the classic prom pose.

"Is this OK?" he asks.

"Yes," I say.

I know that it is an imitation of the cover of issue 54, the beginning of the arc where Green Guarder and Gargantua are stuck in a time bubble alone together for one hundred years and they have the deepest love affair of all time. But then when the bubble bursts, neither of them remembers it. But we the readers do. It's the kind of comic book arc that makes you cry.

So we do one where he's behind me, holding me like we're in a prom photo, and I shift my body a bit to try to look all melodramatic, the way Gargantua does on that cover.

"Great stuff," the photographer says. "Wonderful homage. You guys really nailed it. Just wait here while I print one up."

We get the prints, but the photographer hands us only one of each.

"Can't we get two?" I ask. "So we can each have one?"

"Sorry," he says. "But they'll be online later."

"Do you think that they really hated each other?" Kirk asks. "During the Time War run?"

"Well, they believed in separate solutions. And he did vote to destroy her time line."

"His hands were tied," Kirk says. "Someone was going to suffer."

"But it cost her. It cost them all. I mean, why did it have to be Gargantua's family?"

We argue the results of all the other teams' time lines being removed from time. We're talking over each other, and laughing.

"I don't think the creators knew what they were doing!" Kirk says.

"Yeah, sometimes they are totally making it up as they go along," I laugh. "But I love it."

"Face it, in the end, really Gargantua is the only one who could have survived it," Kirk says.

"It's true," I say. "But it really pitted them against each other for a while."

"Until they fell in love," Kirk says.

There is something about the way he says that, about how easy he is to talk to that catches me off guard as we enter our email address to get a digital copy.

"Which photo do you want?" I ask as we walk out of the booth and back into the fray.

"It doesn't matter," he says.

"I got one yesterday of me and Yuri," I say. "You can pick."

He takes the prom picture issue 54 homage. That surprises me. Not that he picked it. But that once he did, I knew it was the one I wanted.

When I get home that night and de-mask, I tape the picture of me and Kirk up on my mirror. I text Kirk a funny text. But I don't hear back from him. It's weird, because usually he responds right away.

My phone pings, and it's Yuri.

Hey. Here's a list of side characters from Team Tomorrow. How many do you know?

Let's play this game tomorrow, I text back. *Gotta go to bed.*

g'nite

nite

I look at the list and I know them all, but I don't feel like having a long text conversation about how I have to prove it.

Instead, I'm still looking at the picture of Gargantua and Green Guarder taped to my mirror.

I stare at it for a while, examining every detail of the picture. The way Kirk and I are standing. The way our faces look. The way we look like we flow nicely, and by the time I go to bed, my mind begins to spin out.

Does he like me? Does he not like me? What does the way he looked at me in the picture mean? Why hasn't he texted me back? Are we just friends? He's not my type. I'm not his type. Do I have a type? Does he want to kiss me? Do I want to kiss him? Wait, I have a boyfriend.

I'm being weird. Or maybe he's being weird. It was only a weird bubble moment. One that will be forgotten. It probably means nothing at all.

This feeling is so nice/horrible/wonderful/terrible/floaty/rotten.

My heart is on fire. My heart is exploding. My heart is growing. My heart is shrinking.

My heart.

Is so *confused*.

Winter

TEAM TOMORROW
FAN EVENT

One

I used to love the holidays. I used to love road trips. The hours in the car to think or disappear into my phone without being told to put it away. The snacks. Roadside attractions. Staring out the window. But this road trip isn't as much fun. We're not going to be doing touristy stuff in the Bay Area this Christmas. We're going to a hotel way out of town, near the headquarters of the company my dad works for, to cobble together a holiday meal.

Mom, Grandma Jackie, and I check in and get dressed up to have dinner in the hotel restaurant, which is not the most private of places to have a strained family reunion.

Dad looks thin and has dark circles under his eyes and I don't know how to look at him. We awkwardly hug and he places a present in front of me.

"Open it," he says.

I rip the package open and pull out a pair of Team Tomorrow pajamas. They are cozy and soft.

"You don't have them already, do you?" he asks.

"No," I say. "Thanks."

"The new trailer looks pretty good," he says.

It bothers me that my dad is trying to connect with me so hard. It's almost like he's taking this one thing that I love and he's poisoning it.

"Yeah," I mumble, and then bury my head in the menu like I'm really struggling with my choice of entrée. My eyes flit around the hotel. The weird brown décor. The fluorescent lights flickering outside the restaurant.

The adults start talking and I'm sinking lower into my menu, when I hear my dad say something that makes my blood freeze.

"There is going to be a trial and it's possible I will do a little time," my dad says, like it's nothing at all.

Jail.

My dad might go to jail.

The first thing I do is explode. I actually let out a primal scream. It doesn't even sound like me. It's like I'm being born out of myself. The way Gargantua was born when she stepped out of a hardened husk of her old self after being sliced with a neutrino blast while working in the lab.

On the inside, I grow ten feet tall and I scale and harden.

"I wanted this to be a nice Christmas dinner." My mom quietly starts to cry. Her Kleenex dabs the corner of her eyes, as if she can somehow stop the flow of tears. She can't.

"I've got a good lawyer," he says. "And I'm going to get out of this. If I turn myself in before trial, I may be able to cut a deal."

"I thought your special skill was to wiggle your way out of tricky financial situations," my mom says. "I thought this inquiry was the end of it."

"What exactly are they saying?" Grandma Jackie asks calmly. She's always like that, trying to get all the information she can to make the most informed decisions.

"I just don't understand," my mom says over and over again. "I just don't understand."

She's on repeat. She's skipping again. She's spinning out.

"I moved some things and maybe it didn't look so good," he says, almost half nervous laughing, like this whole thing is funny.

It's not funny.

I zone out while he rambles on about a lot of things that I can't or don't want to understand.

"People do it all the time, shuffle things around," he's saying when I tune back in. "I just need to explain it. Clear it up."

Then he flashes the classic Kupferman smile. The one that gets him all the big deals and always gets him out of trouble and makes everyone like him. Except now, suddenly to me, his face looks fake. Like always trying to cut a deal has made him oily.

Maybe that is what bothers me about him being so into Team Tomorrow right now, so that he can put one over on me.

"I'm sorry, kid." He turns to me. "I've made a bit of a mess of things."

"Hollywood people got screwed by your company," I say.

"A lot of people did," he says. "Their payrolls and pensions. I am sorry."

"Well, maybe say it to them, not just to me," I say.

"I'm trying to do just that," he says. "The trial will sort it out. Everything is on hold until this is sorted out," he says.

He says that again, *sorted out*, as though his cooking the books is something you can just hand-wave away. Or like he didn't really do it. Even though he just admitted to us that he definitely did do something.

"When is it going to get *sorted out*?" I say, asking the question that my mom is too afraid to ask.

"Soon," he says. "Look. This is just a blip."

Oh, Gus," my mom says as she blows her nose. "This is not a blip. You've been up here for months."

"It's going to be fine, Mel," he says. "That's why it's good to turn myself in. Makes it smoother."

My mom puts down her tissue, almost as though she believes him and is relieved.

But I can see that there is a small bead of sweat rolling off of my dad's forehead and I know, with a sudden wave of certainty, the real depth of it all.

He is lying.

And this is not going to be quick or easy or smooth. This is going to be *terrible*. And he's not *maybe* going to jail. He's totally going to go to jail.

It's like one of those superhero movies, where everything is collapsing around them in slow motion, like a house of cards, and they are pretending not to see it. Everything is still standing but also completely and utterly destroyed.

My mom and Grandma Jackie start eating mechanically like robots. Maybe we are all robots. That happened once in a trippy run in Team Tomorrow. It turned out at the end of the issue that the whole story that just happened wasn't them but was replicas of the team as androids. They were having these existential crises and it didn't make much sense until the end of the issue when the real team came busting in and had to deactivate them all. That was a good one.

"This is going to get cleared up," Dad says again. "Mark and Bobby and Lawrence and Tyler will help set the record straight."

"Excuse me," I say. I can't listen to him anymore.

I go up to our hotel room and scream into my pillow.

If I could point to a moment in my life so far and say, "This is it. This is the moment that everything changed," I would point to this one. The moment is almost physical. Like it's another person in the room punching me repeatedly.

People often say that change is good. Changing because you want change is one thing. But sudden change that's forced upon you is a ruinous earthquake, and there's not one thing that I can do about it except go unwillingly forward.

Two

E ven though we are on winter break, I am still obliged to
go to the hospital and visit the kids. It's the one thing that
I actually look forward to. It makes me feel like I've got
some kind of spirit. To balance this feeling of goodness, when
I still feel pretty wretched, I start dressing only as villains.

Kirk doesn't join me right after Christmas and he doesn't
reply to any of my texts or emails. At first I think, *Oh, it's just the
holidays*. And then a part of me worries that he hates me and I
didn't know why. And then I feel guilty again because I think
more about not hearing from Kirk than I do about not hearing
from Yuri.

But then, even though he didn't respond, right after New
Year's, there is Kirk standing at the nurses' station dressed as
Batman.

"Hey," he says. "Sorry I didn't give you a heads-up I was
coming. Some stuff came up."

"No," I say. "It's cool. It's the holidays. Family."

"Yeah, family stuff," he says. He runs his hand through

his hair and I am staring at his hand and thinking how nice it looks.

We both look at each other and then look away.

"You didn't make it to the Ferrar twins' New Year's party," I say. I know he was invited because I saw him on the list and it said that he had replied "maybe."

"I did something else," he says, but doesn't elaborate on what. "Was it fun?"

"It was OK," I say. "I went with Yuri."

"Of course," he says. And I kind of blush because being at New Year's with Yuri implies that I was kissing Yuri. Which I was.

"Let's go," I say. "We're in the playroom today."

We go to the playroom and are busily occupied with our handful of kids, so we don't really talk to each other, but still, as before, it feels like we're in this together.

When the day is done, I don't want to stop hanging out with him. I want to go and talk. I jerk my thumb at the diner when we get outside and he nods, and we slide into a booth.

"Kids sure do like to freak out over characters," he says over the fries that I owed him. "They are real nerds."

"Question," I say. "What is your position on fake nerds and real nerds?"

"I think everyone is a nerd about something."

"That's what I think," I say.

I don't say that I am asking because Yuri and his friends make me feel a bit rattled when they question me, and I just want confirmation that they are wrong and I am right.

I wonder if Kirk already knows that.

"That whole fake geek girl thing is dumb," Kirk says. "My mom has been a nerd since time was born."

I like that he uses a Team Tomorrow phrase.

"But people think that," I say. "They test you and they question you. Or they dismiss you and your fandom. It makes me so angry."

"It's the worst," he says. "I'm sorry that you've had to deal with that."

I like that he gets it. That I don't have to explain. Or defend my position. I can just be myself.

It feels like the best of both worlds. Like being good and evil at the same time. Being angry about something but also being glad that it has brought you together with someone.

TEAM TOMORROW

There have been a bunch of rotating members of Team Tomorrow. Team Tomorrow is a band of superheroes that came together after a time schism. They have a bunch of powers. Flying. Strength. Invisibility. True touch. Time bending. Photosynthesis. Growth spurt.

Team Tomorrow's members reflect the strengths that are needed in a society as it grows. They are a true team. Members are added as new things come up in the world. They moved through wars, the civil rights movement, feminism, and threats to democracy.

It's remarkable that at times, the radical nature of the team was dismissed because it was thought of as "just" a comic book.

Comic books, as we know through study, often reflect the anxieties of the times.

Three

I didn't think that going back to school would be weird, but after a winter break, things are somehow different. And because I feel different, I do something radical. I dye my hair Gargantua purple.

"What have you done?" Grandma Jackie says when I come down for breakfast to go to school.

"I felt like I needed a change," I say.

"I think it looks cool; having weird colors isn't like when I grew up," my mom says. "It's more acceptable. Maybe I'll dye my hair, too."

Her roots have been growing out, so she's looking dingy with all that gray hair. Grandma Jackie and I look at each other. It would be a step forward, I think.

"You want some of my purple?" I ask.

My mom smiles. She doesn't laugh, but she smiles.

"I'll let you know," she says.

"Oh my gosh, oh my gosh," Kasumi says, touching my hair when I get to school.

"Well, that's a look," Yuri says. I can't tell if he likes it or hates it.

"Wow. You look like Gargantua," Kirk says as he joins us and we walk into the building after the first bell.

"That's what I was going for," I say.

I feel weird around Kirk now. I can't quite figure it out, and so by the time I am sitting in English class not listening to my teacher talk about Shakespeare, I am thinking about everything. Thinking about why is it that getting closer to someone sometimes makes you feel as though you've gotten further apart?

There is a strange thing that happens between two people sometimes. A moment where everything is cool and easy. You text easily. You email easily. You touch their leg or punch their shoulder easily. And then without warning, something changes.

Suddenly, you feel weird. Your body feels different around them. You think about them too much and then you wonder why. It's such a subtle shift. Because nothing has changed really. You are both exactly the same. But it's different somehow.

You want to tell them something that no one else will understand because you both have a secret language. You have a private joke. You share a thing between you. But instead, you stop texting them. Or talking to them. Or anything, because you don't want to be obvious.

Because when you finally get around to thinking about it, you realize that you like them.

Like them like them.

Four

It's already a few weeks into the new year and Kasumi and I are eating lunch in the quad, and she's asking me questions about what I want to do for my birthday, and I'm trying to deflect her questions and play it like a tiny, low-key thing is what I always wanted, reversing years of conversations we've had.

The sun is out, but it's winter, so it's a little bit cold. But at least it's not rainy. I am trying to talk about the weather and Team Tomorrow and homework, basically just anything else so I can be talking about something other then me.

I'd thought maybe a 1990s-themed ice-skating party, but hiring the rink and DJ for two hours for a private skate is too much. Or a big house party, but I don't want anyone coming over to the house. A day at Disneyland or Universal, but tickets are too expensive for one person, let alone ten or more.

So basically, I'm trying to convince Kasumi that I've always wanted the whole thing to be a chill kind of affair.

I'm trying to pretend that it is not a big deal, but it is a big deal, because I had these big ideas, but instead, I just feel as though the whole thing, like my whole year, is falling flat.

"Oh," Kasumi says, nodding. "I get it. You want a surprise party. I'll talk to your mom."

She says it conspiratorially and like she is going to do the opposite of what I am actually saying to her, because she thinks that's what I mean. And maybe that's what it would have been in the past, for her to do something against my wishes, but not this time.

"No," I say in a panic. "Don't bother her."

Kasumi looks a bit surprised at my reaction. I take a deep breath and figure that maybe I should explain to her what is happening, but instead, Kasumi starts nodding empathetically.

"Because of the separation," Kasumi says. "OK. Low-key."

Her trying to make me happy makes me treasure her most as a friend, but it's misplaced right now and I don't know how to get that across.

"Hey, it's your birthday?" Kirk says. It's like he's been standing there the whole time, but he just walked up. I'm surprised. Sometimes I wonder if he has special morphing powers. He seems to teleport in and around my space all the time.

"Soon," I say. "No big deal."

"She's not having a party," Kasumi says. Then she mouths, *She's probably having a party.*

"What's up, Kirk?" I ask, once again trying to steer the focus away from me.

"I was talking to Yuri and he said the funds were too low to get stuff to make foam weapons."

"Again? That's weird," I say. "We should have money enough for that. I just did that emergency fund collection. I'll talk to him."

It's become my least favorite thing to do, talk to Yuri about club funds. We want to do all these things, take workshops, get materials, go on field trips, but no matter how much we raise, we're always coming up short.

"Well, I can't buy the foam up front and get reimbursed," Kirk says. "'Cause I'm poor."

It makes me uncomfortable that he says that. Not because he's poor. But because I don't know what the word *poor* means anymore. Am I poor? Is he poor? Is Kasumi poor? What is poor? Not eating? Not having a big birthday party? Not having a car? Not buying a new thin sweater? Not having a roof? Not having the stuff to make a cooler costume? There are so many ways to be poor.

"Edan, why don't you front the money?" Kasumi asks. "Work it out with Yuri after."

"I can't front it," I say, and I look at Kasumi. She looks at me quizzically. Then nods.

"Right," she says. "You're on a budget for your secret birth-day thing that you're doing that I can't figure out what it is yet. I can't front any money, either; things are tight right now."

"They are?" I ask. Kasumi's family seems to do pretty well. Her father is so sought after as a cinematographer that he's always going from job to job filming movies. They always seem to have dough to spare. She looks down at her sandwich. When she looks back up, she's got tears in her eyes.

"I don't know. My family is freaking out. My dad's whole investment and retirement got wiped away," she says. "There was some kind of screwup with the last few productions' payroll accounting, so things are on hold. So things are bad at my house."

I go cold.

Could her dad have been caught up in what my dad is involved in? What was it that my mother said, all of Hollywood is interconnected? The company Dad works for does the payments for television shows and movies. Production accounting. Could Kasumi's dad have worked on a film that used their services?

Very likely.

I stand up.

"Where are you going?" Kirk asks. "We still have to figure out foam weapons."

Kasumi's looking up at me like a doe. Sweet and innocent, and I want to puke. I feel funny everywhere. I can't get to the bottom of my dad maybe being involved in harming Kasumi's family. But I can solve the foam.

"I have to find Yuri," I say. "We have to get that foam. I'm going to work it out."

"I'll go with you," Kirk says. He starts to walk with me, but I push him away.

"No," I say.

It's weird, because for me, in that moment, it's as though time freezes. When I'm pushing him away, I really want to bring him in close. I look around the lunch area, the scattered stone picnic tables crowded with kids talking animatedly. The sad-looking mural on the brick wall that some art students are painting. The overflowing garbage cans from where a bird is stealing a piece of bread. It's like each individual moment lasts a thousand years.

I wonder if this is what Gargantua felt when she picked her way through those time-frozen moments.

"OK. See you Saturday?" Kirk asks quizzically.

"Yep," I mumble, trying to make it sound enthusiastic so that he doesn't bail on me. But I think I fail, because I see his eyes go strange and I think, *There he goes*. The moment is passed. I messed this up.

I watch as he leaves and disappears into the door that I know leads to the library.

"That was weird." Kasumi raises her eyebrow at me. "What's going on Saturday?"

"It's nothing," I say. "A study thing."

I don't know why I keep lying to her. I guess that what we do at the hospital is between me and Kirk, and I don't want her to know about it. I feel as though Kirk and I are connected in a way I've never been with anyone else. Like I've got a secret ally. A delicious, wonderful secret just for me. I feel like I can navigate anything when I'm alone with him. In the library during free period, we sometimes sit across from each other, our hands working on math problems or homework, our eyes doing all the talking.

It's not something I want to share. Because it's not something I can explain. I can feel Kasumi staring, like she knows there is more to the story here. But I can't tell her that I want to go somewhere and freak out. That I have to be alone to sort out things. That I don't know how to confide in her that maybe it's my father's fault that her father is having troubles. That I hate every single thing.

"How's Yuri?" she asks, almost like she knows that I'm hiding something.

"He's fine," I say. "I gotta go meet him now, actually."

I head inside to my locker and my hands shake as I open it. There is nothing in there that I need. It's just a place to stick my head in, like an ostrich sticking it's head in the sand.

After breathing for a minute, I feel better.

TEAM TOMORROW

The Fifty Most Important Superheroes

With the upcoming big box office superhero films coming this summer, *Entertainment Today!* has ranked all of your favorite superheroes in order of power. We gathered our geeky experts and came up with some criteria to determine the fifty most important and iconic superheroes of our times.

We judged on influence, relevance, powers, timelessness, character design, persona, and impact. How does your favorite superhero measure up? Do they make the list?

#47 GARGANTUA—Team Tomorrow.

As far as iconic women who date back to the start of comics, there are only a handful. Wonder Woman is the most famous, but Gargantua from Team Tomorrow should not be overlooked. Greer Gorman, a scientist at a time when scientists were nearly all men, held her own as the smartest lady in the room. Her powers, growing and shrinking to size, while they do echo elegantly the idea of female rage, do not manifest from a place of rage, such as is the case with the Hulk. Instead, Gargantua has a more subtle, emotional connection to her power. Her emotional state influences it, but she is able to control it, much like women learn to brighten and fade in any given room. At a time when women were told to be quiet things, Gargantua's ability to make herself known in a room was radical. Not only is she a worthy contemporary of Wonder Woman, but she had style and flair. Gargantua, in her purple, black, and silver, was rarely drawn in any objectifying way. Her costume was always practical and fashion-forward, and while always drawn with an ample bust, that feature was never the center of attention. We hope that with the upcoming *Team Tomorrow* movie that others will rediscover the amazing Gargantua, who, while created in the days of yore, feels fresh and relevant in the twenty-first century.

five

Saturday comes and Kirk doesn't show up. I text him a bunch of times, but he just texts back a cold *Sorry.*

I can't blame him for being weird when I was being weird. I pretty much think he's avoiding me and that's OK. I figure I will apologize to him when we're back at school and then everything will be all right.

I arrive at school on Monday ready with my explanations, but he doesn't show up to school. I text him that I want to meet him in the library, but on Tuesday he doesn't show. Because I don't hear back from him and he didn't show up, I don't want to reach out to him again because I don't want to bother him. And I figure that he's mad at me. But not reaching out to him makes me miserable. Which makes my desire to reach out to him a million times more urgent.

He's not in school. I don't see him in the hallways. I don't see him online. He hasn't posted on social media. It's as though he's disappeared.

I fill my time hanging out with Yuri at his house, playing video games, but I am preoccupied.

By Thursday, Kirk still doesn't show up, and I start to ask around for his schedule and hover around where I think he might be. I stop thinking that maybe he's avoiding me and wonder if maybe something is going on with him.

But the weird thing is that even though he hasn't been around, it's like he's standing right next to me. Or like there is an after-impression of him behind my eyes when I close them.

When Monday comes, and he's still not in school, and it's the start of spring break, I break down and send him a quick text that I'll be volunteering at the hospital again and that I'm looking forward to seeing him. I immediately kick myself for texting him and hours later, when I still don't hear back from him, I feel even weirder. But at the core, all I can think is that I want to see Kirk on Saturday. I want to apologize.

We'll be dressed up as superheroes and I will talk to him over French fries. I will tell him about everything. I will let everything spill out over the table. Maybe he'll nod and tell me it's going to be OK, and I'll be able to face another day at school. Another week. My whole life. I feel like if I don't talk to him soon, I may never go to school again.

But Saturday comes and Kirk doesn't show up at the hospital. And it baffles me because now his silence and absence are so big. So when I get home, I rifle through the club papers and I find his address on his form, which feels a little stalkery, but

I don't care. I have had enough. I don't care about being coy or shy or anything. I am all emotions. I am all about needing what I need right now. Sunday, bright and early, I leave a note telling my family I'm going out and I head over to his house.

He doesn't live in my neighborhood but just next to it. His house is a little worn down, but it's adorable. A real old Hollywood single-family house from 1925.

I knock on the door. And then realize that I have no excuse to be there. No reason, except that I have a burning need to talk to him.

An older woman answers the door. She's younger than my grandmother. Older than my mother. And cooler-looking than both of them. I know I've seen her at the park, but I feel like I've seen her before somewhere else, but I can't place where. She's got silver hair that hangs long down her shoulders and dark, rich blue fringed on the bottom. She's got sleeve tattoos. She's obviously just hanging around the house, but somehow she looks glamorous.

"Hello?" she says, looking me up and down.

"Oh, I'm looking for Kirk," I say.

"He's in the garage," she says. "You're a friend from school?"

"Yes," I say. "We're in a club together."

I look toward the garage and point to it.

She nods.

"Wait, bring this to him," she says. "He's not been eating."

She disappears inside and then comes back with a tray of food and a pitcher of lemonade. She's put two glasses on the tray.

I take the tray and carefully make my way over to the garage, which I notice is open. I put the tray down on a table and marvel at what I'm seeing. There are racks and racks of clothing. Vintage clothing that has been geekified. Geek fabrics cleverly stitched in. I run my hand along the pieces of clothing. I've seen these before. I've been amongst these dresses, wanting every single piece. I know it when I see the Team Tomorrow dress I coveted hanging on a mannequin.

I emerge from the racks to the back of the garage. Kirk is sitting there, at a sewing machine, altering a piece of clothing. My heart is beating really fast. I'm nervous about disturbing Kirk, he is so in a moment.

I watch him silently for a minute. I like the way his tongue touches the corner of his mouth as he concentrates. I like the way his body looks intense. I like the way the sunlight falls on his face.

He stops the line and pulls the fabric up and holds it up to examine it. That's when he looks up and sees me.

"Hey," I say.

"What are you doing here?" he asks.

"I brought you lemonade," I say.

He looks at me; he knows the reason I'm here is so much bigger than that. I'm here because I think that he can really see me when I don't know that I can see myself anymore. I'm here because I'm vulnerable and hurting and in need of someone who can understand me. I'm here because that is a beautiful thing to feel about someone.

"It's over there. Your mom gave it to me."

He gets up and passes me by and goes to the table and pours us both lemonade. He hands me a glass.

"That was my grandma," he says. "My mom is resting."

We drink in silence. The lemonade is delicious and I can see a tree in the yard that is bursting with lemons. It is sweet and tart, matching how I feel about sitting here with him.

"What is this place?" I say. "It's like a magical land of amazing things."

"It's my mom's business," he says.

"She makes nerd-inspired clothes?" I ask.

He nods and takes a bite out of his sandwich.

"They have a booth at cons," I say, piecing it all together.

He nods.

"You haven't been at school," I say. "I thought I'd see you this week, but now it's break and I wanted to say I'm sorry about being weird."

He mumbles something I can't hear.

"What?" I ask, scooting in closer to him.

"I can't be there for everyone," he says.

"I know," I say. "I just wanted to hang out and you weren't there."

"I'm trying to keep up with the orders. Help my mom out."

"Have you been working here all week? Is she exploiting you?" I try to make it sound like a joke. But it falls flat and he looks at me with a hard, pained look.

"Why do you think I was at the hospital that first Saturday?" he asks.

"To help me," I say. "Because I asked."

"To be there for my mom because she had an appointment for some tests," he says.

I flash back to when I saw him standing with two coffee cups. It hits me all at once.

"Cancer?"

"Yeah," he says. "Stage four. Ovarian."

"Oh, Kirk. I'm so sorry."

"It's not going well," he says. "They keep doing procedures and tests and treatments, but it feels like nothing is working. I want to get things done for her. Make her feel like her business stuff is taken care of. That all of this will continue when . . ."

He doesn't have to finish the sentence. It might not be soon, but he knows what's coming and so do I.

We both sit there.

"My dad is going to go on trial and I think he's going to go to jail," I say. "And I think that he's going to be there for a very long time."

He looks at me like he's seeing me anew. At first I feel so vulnerable and exposed. But then his look softens.

"I'm sorry, Edan," he says.

Then he puts the sandwich down and puts his fists to his eyes. His shoulders hunch up. And he shudders a bit. He's so quiet about it. I can hardly hear anything. But I know he's crying.

I don't know why I do it, but I do.

I put my arms around his waist and pull him close to me.

He resists for a second but then sinks into me. He slides his arms around me and puts his face into my shoulder and he sobs.

I whisper to him. And then I kiss his cheek. And his neck. And his ear.

And then before I know what I'm doing, I'm kissing Kirk Gomez.

And it's the best kiss that I've ever had in my life.

I am in Kirk's arms and it feels exactly right where I'm supposed to be. We are in the corner couch in the garage, lounging and entwined in each other's arms, and I don't want this moment to ever end. I only want to be looking in his eyes. I only ever want to touch his hands. I only ever want to hear his voice low and near me.

The kissing that we do in between is achingly perfect. And I know in a flash that this kiss is not like any kiss I've ever had with Yuri. But more so, it's the talking that I enjoy so much. The absolute best part about liking somebody is the sharing. The whispering. The holding. The kissing. The being with him.

"How did your mom start the business?" I ask when we are just sitting there on the couch, comfortably in each other's arms.

"When you are a nerd, you find a way that being a nerd can make you money," he says. "My mom just made nerdy clothes for herself to go to cons with. Then her friends commissioned her. Then strangers. Then she started tabling."

"I want to own everything in your garage," I say.

Kirk laughs.

"That's why my mom makes the big bucks now," he says.

"You are right," I say. "I mean, look at cosplaying. People make that their living now."

"Yeah," Kirk says. "It's a geek's world right now."

When I finally leave a few hours later, nothing is settled. I don't know that what happened is anything more than an isolated bubble universe.

Gargantua had many of those kinds of moments.

They meant everything and they meant nothing.

Six

When Monday comes, I think for sure that when I see Kirk, it will be weird and wonderful. But instead it's as though nothing has happened.

"Hey," he says when we pass each other in the hallway. But there is no longer that special something that always seemed to pass between us. It's like we're hot and cold.

"Oh, hey!" I say, casual-like. No big deal. Things just back the way they were. By Friday, the kiss has been forgotten because it changed nothing. Maybe even made things slightly worse.

"You OK?" Kasumi asks me as we re-dye my hair purple and put blond streaks into her hair at her house on Friday night for a sleepover. "You've seemed low all week."

"Did you ever think that it would be great to have a super-power like reading someone's mind?"

"Oh my gosh, yes," Kasumi says as she helps me put a plastic bag over my head to keep the purple dye warm. I help her tinfoil the bleach onto her hair.

"Sometimes I just can't tell what people are thinking, or why they do what they do," I say. "It would be handy to translate their actions and their thoughts."

"I know," she says. "I mean, how do you know if someone likes you?"

"Exactly," I say. "Even when you know they like you, because they must like you, but then it's weird because they don't seem like they like you."

"Right," Kasumi says. "For example, if a girl gives you a Valentine's Day card, and then hangs out with you all the time but doesn't actually say anything, then what does it mean? Does she like you?"

Then I smile, knowing that she's talking about Sophie.

"So you and Sophie?" I say.

Kasumi blushes and laughs, "Maybe? I can't tell!"

And I know exactly how she feels.

"I don't know," I say. "If you have a boyfriend who is your actual boyfriend, but you have to prove over and over that you like the things you like. Do you think they will ever actually believe you are the nerd you say you are?"

"Oh, is Yuri doing that thing again?" Kasumi asks.

"Yeah," I say.

"That's just Phil and Tze talking through him, and they are lame," Kasumi says. "My advice is to get him alone and go somewhere nice and geek out with him. He really likes you. He says it all the time."

"I just feel as though if someone likes you, then they know that you like what you like," I say.

"Absolutely," Kasumi says. "I think maybe having things in common and having respect is a big deal. You have to be proactive with Yuri. Show him how to treat you next week for your birthday. Drop big hints."

"You going to be proactive with Sophie?" I ask.

Kasumi blushes and then throws her arms up in the air.

I take Kasumi's advice to heart and I email Yuri to remind him that it's my birthday and that since I'm not going to do anything big for it, I want to do something geeky with him.

He texts back a Vulcan live-long-and-prosper emoji, so I'm pretty sure he gets the point.

When my birthday comes around, I get to school and Kasumi has decorated my locker, and that makes me feel really great except that Yuri doesn't know why she did it.

"What's all this?" he asks, pointing at the fancy ribbons and stuff.

"It's my birthday, remember?" I say. I point to the *Happy Birthday* sign.

"Oh, man," he says. "Kidding! How lame would I be for not knowing, especially after your text?"

"Pretty lame," I say.

He laughs and pulls me in for a hug.

"I have it all arranged for us to go to Universal Studios this weekend and Harry Potter it up or something. I've got passes."

He kisses me again as the bell rings.

"OK," I say. And I know I should be really happy. I am getting exactly what I wanted. But I'm not really feeling it. I am looking over his shoulder. I am avoiding his eyes and his hands.

But I like him. Don't I? So what is this feeling like I am being pulled elsewhere?

I walk into English class depressed. It didn't have to be a perfect birthday, but I needed it to feel a little bit special. I'm getting increasingly bummed out by Yuri. It's like he looks good on paper, and he does a lot of the right things, but there is something not quite there in the flesh. I feel upside down about my heart. As though it is a bit like cosplaying having these feelings for him.

There is a hand on my shoulder. I turn.

"Hey." It's Kirk. He's followed me into my classroom.

"What are you doing here?" I ask. Half hoping that maybe he transferred into this class or something. Why else would he be here?

"Happy birthday," he says.

I look at him and he's got a shit-eating grin on his face. It's so different from the cold and aloof Kirk that I've been passing in the hallways for the past week.

"What?" I say.

He pulls out his phone and shows me.

"This is your present," he says. "If I can pull it off."

And there, in the form of a press release on the Internet is one of the most amazing things I've ever seen. It's an announcement for a *Team Tomorrow Fan Event*.

In a few weeks, there is going to be an event at the studio with a new trailer. It will include an interview with the cast, a pop-up comic book shop with the first wave of toys, and a party at the studio lot.

"What?" I say. "I have to go to this."

"I'm working on it," Kirk says. "No guarantees. But I'm working on it. I might have an in, but I'm also going to sign up for every contest. Every ticket giveaway. You have to as well, just to play all the odds."

He's still standing there smiling at me.

I know it's not like I'm actually going yet to the fan event. Or that the fan event was made for me. But somehow it feels like it was. As though the universe wanted to give me one piece of good news that I could hang on to.

"It's going to be impossible to get, but I'll ask Kasumi about it as well," I say. "You'd need to know someone or know someone who knows someone. Or be someone. Or kill someone."

"There's gotta be a way," he says. "I'm determined. I'll use my powers of the sun."

"I'll grow a million feet tall," I say.

"Anything, my liege," he says, and does the flourish.

"Don't play with me," I tease him. "I will be crushed."

I want to hug him, because even his just telling me about it is like a birthday present. But hugging seems weird. Because I don't even know if our kissing counted. So instead we awkwardly high-five.

And while it's not a birthday present that I can wear or hold, it's a birthday present that I can feel in my heart.

Someone is working really hard to try to make me happy.

I want to talk more. To ask about his mom, but before he can say anything else, the bell rings and my English teacher interrupts as he starts the class.

"Everyone who is in this class should be sitting. Anyone who isn't should be in a different place," my English teacher says.

Kirk just kind of hangs there for a moment more, as if there is something frozen in the air and out there that he wants to say and he doesn't know how to put it back.

"Were you going to say something else?" I ask. I feel he wants to tell me something important. But instead of saying anything, I watch as the thought fades and he gets whatever he's feeling under control.

"Sorry if I've been a bit weird," he says quickly. "It's been hard at home and I can't figure out how to balance everything. I just can't hang out with anyone right now. You understand, right?"

When he says that, I know he's not going to confess that he has feelings for me or anything. Which I'm both glad and not glad about. Because that would be awkward. And I would have to reject him until I sorted out things with Yuri.

"You're going to get a late mark," I say.

"Worth it for the look on your face about the fan event," he says.

Then it hits me like a ton of bricks.

I have to break up with Yuri.

Seven

After walking through Universal Studios, after he buys me a wand and some butterbeer, after riding three roller coasters, I break up with Yuri while we're eating sushi.

"What do you mean you're breaking up with me?" he asks. "Are you playing with me? Is this some kind of a joke?"

"No, I'm not playing with you," I say.

"Then what?" he asks. "Then why?"

"I am going through a lot right now and I just want to be alone," I say.

"This is crap," he says.

But it's just that I don't want to be with him. He's not the right team member for me.

"It's about me, not you," I say.

I have heard that in movies and never thought I'd actually say something like that. And it strikes me that really it's both. It's me and it's him.

"Why'd you let me waste these tickets on you?" he asks.

"I didn't think it was a waste," I say. "It was my birthday. I wanted to come, but things have changed."

"Are you kidding me? You make me be nice to you all day and then you dump me?"

"I didn't make you be nice to me," I say.

"You know you are lucky that I even went with you because I don't know any other guy who would go for all of your weirdness," he says.

"My what?" I ask.

"I mean, look at your hair? What is that?"

"It's nice," I say. "It looks like Gargantua. Makes my cosplay more real."

"About that. You let it all hang out at Comic Con, but you don't let me touch you," he says. "You're just a tease."

"What?" I say.

"You are, like, a girl that pretends to be all cool and into stuff, but you really aren't. You just use it to hook boys."

"What?"

"Girls like you," he says. "You pretend to be into stuff, learn to talk the talk. Hooking up with boys, invading our spaces."

I never really thought that he was so much like Phil, but it's obvious he feels exactly like Phil. I always hand-waved it away, because somehow he seemed different with me when we were alone, but it's as though he was always wearing a mask and pretending with me. And now I'm seeing the ugly creature below.

"I think you're taking this badly, but it's just that I am at a different place than I was last summer," I say, trying not to clobber him. "I have a lot going on."

"You're not even that hot," he says. Then he starts to list things that he thinks are physically ugly about me.

"And you're going to be sorry."

He curses me out some more and then gets up and leaves. I sit there for a while and then I get the rest of my sushi to go. I realize I don't have a ride home. I don't want to call my mom or Grandma Jackie, so I hike down the hill and take the metro home, which takes forever but gives me a lot of time to think.

When I get in the door, there are birthday pancakes and Grandma sticks a candle in them for me to blow out because she and Mom were so busy with the news that the case against my dad was going to trial, they kind of forgot on the actual day. My mom comes out of her room to sing "Happy Birthday" to me, and I realize that is pretty huge and likely the only present I'm going to get from her.

I try to be grateful. I really do.

But what I'd really like is for her to wake up and do something. Like give me advice about breaking up with my first boyfriend. Like hugging me and telling me that it's going to be OK. Like telling me that I didn't just mess up my life with a boy who liked me for a boy who maybe doesn't even care.

I'm not hungry because I am full with thoughts of dread about how Yuri reacted. I have this feeling in the pit of my stomach like this isn't going to be easy.

226

It doesn't even take him that long to start making life miserable for me and making good on his threat that I will be sorry. First it's him texting me every ten minutes telling me how horrible I am. Horrible-looking. Horrible kisser. Horrible personality. Horrible everything. About how I'm the worst. About how I'm frigid. By the time I am ready for bed, Yuri has gone full-on ballistic and I'm exhausted.

Then he starts posting pictures of me and makes memes of them about how I'm a fake geek girl. He posts them everywhere. And by everywhere, I know it's probably not actually everywhere, but it feels like everywhere relevant to me.

These things hurt the most. Even though I know it's not true and he's just needling me, it works. It gets under my skin. And I wonder how I got here.

It's a nasty end.

I'm crying into my pillow when my phone pings.

Are you ok? Kirk texts me. Kirk attaches a picture of me as a meme. It's me in my Gargantua outfit. It says "Flabby and Small."

I broke up with Yuri, I text back.

I figured, he says.

It totally sucks, I reply.

I hope it's not because of what happened, he says.

That makes me feel worse. Of course it was partly because of him. Because he made me feel when I wasn't feeling. Because I could see what liking someone who really gets me could be like.

Of course not, I say. *Not you. All me. I'm the villain.*

It's a lie, but it makes me feel better.

:D, he texts back. It reads to me as though he's relieved.

The . . . hangs for a bit and finally a new text comes up.

Remember when Team Tomorrow tried a new tactic to desta-bilize Gargantua and keep her in line? he texts. *Undermine her confidence?*

Yeah, I say.

Don't let him do that to you, he says. *Be Gargantuan.* Gotta go, good night.

Good night.

Be Gargantuan.

Eight

When I get to school, everyone is looking at me. When I pass people in the hallway, they snicker and say things under their breath. I can't help but wonder about all the things that I don't know Yuri is saying about me. I shudder and try not to think about it.

"You OK?" Kasumi asks me as we open up the the costume room for a club meeting.

"I don't know," I say. "Everything seems hard."

"Tough to break up with someone," she says. "I mean I wouldn't know, but I can guess."

We both sigh.

"Well, I'm just trying to concentrate on getting those Team Tomorrow fan tickets," I say.

"My dad is trying, but honestly, it doesn't look good," Kasumi says.

"Someone has got to have an in," I say. "I hear they're giving exclusive swag."

"My dad keeps telling me not to bother him about it. He's working with a bunch of other below-the-line people to sue the production company for nonpayment."

"Right," I say. Nonpayment. Probably because of what my dad did. I keep seeing in the papers and online that unions are planning to sue the accounting company.

"Yeah," she says.

"Oh, hi, Sophie!" I nudge Kasumi, who changes her whole demeanor when Sophie comes in the room. I am grateful for the interruption because it helps me to avoid the subject of her dad and my dad.

Sophie comes over to us with a big garment bag.

"What's that?" Kasumi asks, but it's really like she's saying, *I like you I like you I like you.*

"We had some spare damaged garments from storage," Sophie says to us, but she's looking at Kasumi. "I thought your club could use them since we can't. Maybe we could trade for some portraits of our cast."

Kasumi blushes and takes the garment bag.

"Thanks, Sophie," Kasumi says. And I notice *a look* passes between them. Sophie likes Kasumi as much as Kasumi likes Sophie.

The other club members come in and Sophie leaves, so we don't really get a private chance to talk, but I give Kasumi a look that says, *She likes you.* And Kasumi gives me a look back that says, *I know!*

To my surprise and horror, Yuri shows up to the club

meeting with Tze. But Kirk doesn't show up. He's conspicu-
ously absent.

I start the meeting and suffer through Yuri making horrible
comments every time I speak. He mocks my voice. He makes a
sarcastic remark. He vetoes every motion I put forth. He makes
fun of my mask, my hair, my figure, my everything. No one speaks
up. Kasumi just keeps looking at me helplessly.

How come it's so hard to come to someone's rescue?

How come it's so hard to come to your own rescue?

TEAM TOMORROW

You can see in the panel placement of Gargantua and Green Guarder that they are constantly placed in positions of equality.

When there is a gaze from either the audience or from character to character, both are admiring the other excelling in their element. In their form.

Gargantua, although for many issues an enemy, always remarks on the Green Guarder, always showing him absolute admiration.

Green Guarder always extends an olive branch, which is always rebuked. But he persists. He is often framed watching her form as she leaves.

This equality that Gargantua and Green Guarder maintain with each other in the sequential art is something that each creative team has continued throughout every iteration of the series.

Nine

You can't hide from the news.

Before Kasumi and I can make a plan to have a big, long heart-to-heart over the weekend so I can tell her everything in my own way, my whole life goes public. I had thought Yuri making fake geek girl memes about me and leading a character assassination of me at school and online was bad, but that was nothing.

The news about my dad is everywhere. It's there on the television. Radio. Twitter. Facebook. People share the links. And repost. And you cannot hide from the twenty-four-hour news cycle. It is relentless and aggressive. You are exposed.

My dad's name is in CAPITAL LETTERS everywhere. And then people start posting on my wall. "Is this you?" "Is this your dad?" And I cannot hide under a bed. Or under a pillow. Or under a mask. I am revealed. And what I feel like is like I am a thing worse than a bug under a magnifying glass. Even though I am referred to as "teenage daughter," it does not provide anonymity in my own microcosm. I am exposed now for being a liar. For having kept a secret.

And even though you feel very small and full of shame, you end up being gargantuan. Because everyone is staring at you. All eyeballs. They are whispering about you. All mouths moving. They are listening to you. All ears leaning in.

But the worst is when your best friend confronts you.

Kasumi arrives at my house to pick me up for our hangout and I can tell immediately that nothing is going to go the way I wanted. I waited too long. I am too late. She is standing on the porch in front of me, holding her phone to my face with the news. And instead of her being sympathetic and comforting me as she has for the past week about the memes, she's full of fury.

"Is it true?" she asks.

Her eyes are red-rimmed. Her eyes have a look I've never seen before. I think it's about my dad. And how he may have affected her dad's life. But upon closer inspection of the phone, it's a document with the SEW club dues. An exposé of sorts, where it looks like I have been wiggling money around and pocketing cash and making mysterious transfers.

"Did you steal money from our club?" she asks.

"What?" I ask. "What are you talking about?"

She hands me the phone, and I scroll through and I see a bunch of posts that have picture snapshots of me shuffling money around in PayPal. Emails to Yuri about giving him cash. Numbers that I've never seen before.

And when I look at all of that on paper, I can see that it looks as though I have betrayed SEW.

"No," I say. "It's not what it looks like."

"Well, it looks pretty bad," Kasumi says. "Like you were short on cash and took some for yourself."

"That's Yuri," I say. "He's the treasurer."

"He's not the one making all of these deposits and withdrawals."

And I realize I have been set up. And I can't defend myself because I look guilty. And my father's crime, now public, makes it all the easier to believe that I am like him.

When that happens in a story, it is like *whoa*. You are telescoped out and you can see it all. But when it happens in your own life, it is completely shocking.

"Who are you?" she asks.

"It wasn't me," I say. "I didn't do this. You know how Yuri has it out for me right now."

"Yeah, he does, as a stupid boy, but this is dollars and cents. This is real, not just him making stuff up."

"I didn't do this," I say. "Remember at the movies, with the candy, I gave him cash. Maybe he took it? Maybe it didn't all go in."

"No, look at these emails," she says. "These log-ins from your account."

"I gave him my password to make things easier," I say. "It wasn't me."

"You know me," I say, appealing to her as my best friend of many years.

"Do I?" she asks. "You didn't tell me about your dad, and now this?"

And there it is. The thing that I wanted to tell her and should have and didn't. And now it looks like I have something more to hide.

Then I get a bit angry, but not because I'm mad about it, but because I've been so wrapped up in my stuff that I haven't been paying attention to Kasumi's stuff.

When Gargantua left the Team Tomorrow fold, she forgot about a lot of things. And even though she thought she was trying to make things better by removing herself from her world, she made things worse.

Maybe if she had ever figured out how to find that one time thread and go back, she wouldn't have messed things up.

"I wanted to tell you," I say. "I was going to tell you. I just didn't know how."

"You knew my dad was probably affected," she says. "I cried to you about it. You should have told me."

I can't argue with her. She's right. I wish I had the power to go back to tomorrow and change today.

"I was embarrassed, and when I found out that maybe he'd hurt you, I was mortified."

"Edan, I'm sorry," she says. "I don't think I want to hang out with you for the next little while."

"Come on, Kasumi," I say. "Don't freeze me out."

But it's like I'm Green Guarder begging Gargantua to not leave. Impossible.

Kasumi looks at me and then closes her eyes slowly. She just stands there, silent with her eyes closed. She's not even crying, she's just like a statue. And that is what gets me the most scared, because she's so calm.

"I'm sorry, Kasumi," I say. "I'm going to fix this. We're friends. We're *best* friends."

She snaps her eyes open and looks right at me. Right in me. Right down me. She's got a superpower in her *look*; it is the power of thinking you've found the truth.

"Don't call me your *best* friend anymore," she says. Then she turns and leaves me standing by myself. I collapse to my smallest state and watch her retreating body.

I messed things up by keeping things from her all this time. I look guilty and I feel guilty even though I'm not guilty.

I'm a girl without a tomorrow. I'm a girl with a bad yesterday. I'm a girl with a terrible now.

Ten

Heroes fix their own problems. They shoulder the burden of it and then they attack it head-on, even when the odds are against them. That is what I've learned from comic books, so I try to do the same.

When I get to school, I walk tall. I nod hello to everyone who turns away from me. I try not to take it personally when people dash down corridors and turn about-face when they see me.

The first thing I muster up my courage for is to confront Yuri.

I find him outside, playing hoops with some boys.

"Yuri," I say, trying to keep my voice totally steady, even though I think I'm going to crack. "We need to talk."

"I don't think so," he says. "I don't talk to criminals."

"I don't know what happened and I'm sure there is an explanation," I say. "I was hoping that we could figure it out together."

"It's pretty obvious what happened," he says. "The evidence doesn't lie."

"I didn't steal any money," I say. "I wasn't the treasurer."

"Are you accusing me?" he says, bouncing the ball so that it bounces right near me. I can feel it whizzing by me. His friends are hanging back, observing. Snickering. I have the distinct feeling I am in an evil lair. It makes me appreciate how brave heroes have to be to go somewhere they know they will be attacked.

"I'm not accusing you," I say. "I just want to figure it out so that I can repair whatever happened."

He comes over to me and picks up the ball. He leans in close.

"I don't help villains," he says. He turns and bounces the ball in, and the boys start playing, and the conversation is over.

It's a club day, so I head to the costume room early. I have things prepared that I want to say to the group.

Nadine, Joss, Gwen, and the others start rolling in and they kind of don't know what to do. I say hello to each one of them. They just go and grab whatever it is that they were working on and take a seat.

Kasumi finally comes in; she's talking with Sophie and they are both laughing and holding hands. She sees me and stops. Then looks around like she's looking for someone else. Kasumi is making a big show of not looking at me. It's weird how not looking at someone is like looking at them.

"Hi," I say. "I thought that maybe I could address the club since I think there has been a misunderstanding."

"You can't be in SEW anymore," Kasumi says. "We had an emergency club vote."

"That's a little extreme, don't you think?" I say. "Can't there be an inquiry or something?"

As much as my life is going into the toilet, I am not expecting the club to confront me as hard as they do. They are all in various states of costume; it's like I'm standing in a superhero tribunal.

No one looks up from what they are doing. Joss quietly leaves the room. Everyone is there but Kirk. He seems to be nowhere. Maybe he's just really good at being invisible. There is a part of me that wants to reach out to him, but also, it hits me. He probably voted against me as well. And he hasn't tried to reach out to me. I'd rather be alone than desperate. Even though I feel desperate. I'm determined to defend myself.

"It seems as though there has been a misappropriation of club funds," I say. One or two people look up for a second. I wonder if they think I'm going to confess. I wish I could confess; then at least there would be a way to fix something. But since I didn't do it, I can't.

"Where's the money, Edan?" Gwen asks.

"I don't know," I say. "Yuri is treasurer."

"He quit the club today," Kasumi says. "And when I asked him about it, he said that he transferred all the funds to the club account a few weeks ago, but when I checked, the account was empty."

"He never told me that," I say.

"It has your signature," she says, holding up her tablet to show me.

"That's my name, but not my signature," I say.

"It is," she says.

"No, that's someone's finger squiggle, but not mine," I say.

"Look," Gwen says. "The apple doesn't fall too far from the tree."

"What's that supposed to mean?" I ask.

"It means that your dad embezzled money," Kasumi says. "So why wouldn't you?"

I suck my breath in. This can't be happening. But it is.

"No," I say.

"Give us the money back," Gwen says. "And we can call it a day."

"I don't have that kind of money," I say.

"Then you have to go. We voted to kick you out of the club," Nadine says. "So you have to go."

"But it's *my* club," I say.

"That's the thing; a club is a group, not an individual."

Everyone in the room is staring at me and not helping me. I look around for any friendly face, but they are all stone cold and hard. I realize that Kirk is not there to lift me up with his secret way of doing, so I'm really there all alone.

"I'm going to straighten this out," I say.

"Miss Kupferman." I hear a voice. It's Mrs. Grant, the club faculty advisor. "You're going to have to vacate the premises."

"But I didn't do what they are accusing me of," I say. "I want to address the problem."

She comes up to me and gently leads me out of the costume room.

"You're going to have to go home," she says. She looks like she feels bad for me. "We're already bending the rules by not taking action against you, because of your special difficult circumstances."

"I know it looks bad," I say.

There is no solace there. My eyes keep looking around for the missing Kirk. With Kasumi out of the picture, there was only one person who might understand and help me navigate this whole thing, but he's not around.

I can see Kasumi standing in the doorway, watching what is going on as I am talked to by Mrs. Grant. I wish she would step out and talk to me. I wish she would let me explain how it's impossible that I did it. Even though I don't know how to explain it. I wonder if that is how my dad feels? As though he got caught in something bigger than him and now he's unable to make his way out of it.

I suppose the difference is that he really did something, and I suspect I only accidentally enabled someone to do it. For the very first time, I feel a pang of empathy for the situation he's in.

I go home because I don't know what else to do.

My room is my lair. And I feel evil.

Eleven

"Do you want to skip school and come to the trial with us?" Grandma Jackie asks, coming into my room. She thinks that everything I am being emotional about is because of my dad. And it's funny, because it is and it isn't.

"No," I say. But I don't want to be at school, either.

My mother and grandmother have been going to the trial every day. I get updates on my phone, which I check constantly when I can at school. The big news this week is that his partners have sold him out. He is taking the fall and it doesn't look so good. They all have plausible deniability and he has none.

One week turns into two, and then the weeks go by and it feels like the whole thing, my whole life, is crawling by like centuries. I'm only glad that we are creeping closer and closer to summer break so that I can stop feeling miserable on a daily basis. Grandma Jackie is trying to keep everything normal at home despite how south the trial is going. Grandma Jackie and mom are always there when I get home and she has ordered dinner and set the table. My mother is a ghost at the table. Soon she will disappear, she is so translucent. I am a ghost at the lunch table at school. Becoming thinner by the silent treatment I get every day.

Kasumi and I aren't talking to each other. It's been weeks now and it feels terrible. We pass each other at school and she just crosses the quad or turns around and heads in another direction.

Brutal.

I tried texting her a few times. To tell her that I didn't take the club money, but I stop after I hear nothing back, because there is nothing that makes a person look more guilty than overtexting. I have to deal with the fact that no one wants to believe me.

With no Kasumi around, I have no one to tell me that I'm being ridiculous.

Somehow, even though he thinks I did it, I am brave enough to email Kirk the truth. I show him what I found about how Yuri framed me. Even though it looks desperate. I need Kirk to believe me.

But I get no response.

My feeling is that if you confess a big thing to someone, they should at least ping you back. With an acknowledgment. With a *got it*. Or *yeah*. Or *uh-huh*. Or something.

And the silence is the thing that makes me cry the hardest. Like trying still meant there was hope that Kirk would understand.

Then I wonder if I allowed it to happen. If I am guilty by liking Yuri and not following up with him about things that seemed strange. In a way, I let it slide. Like my dad did. He just turned a blind eye and allowed nefarious things to be done and he got caught and is paying for it.

But I know that if I had known, I would have said something. Because I don't want to be like my dad at all.

It's like when Gargantua didn't express her feelings for Green Guarder for that one arc. She bottled it all up and said nothing. And then, when it finally burst out of her, it came out like a violent energy that destroyed things in its path. What could have helped her became something that harmed her.

The worst thing about losing a friend is seeing how great their life is on social media. I read somewhere that we curate our lives online. That we show only our best parts. And how you have to take it all with a grain of salt. Stuff still is going on behind the scenes. People can post a pic of a happy-looking day and have sobbed in the shower. I certainly do it.

The only reason I know that one day Kasumi and I might be friends again is that she did not unfriend me. She did not block me. She may have hidden me. But I'm not unfollowed. Sure, I have no idea if she's seeing anything that I am doing. Although to be honest, I don't post much lately. I do an occasional geeky craft project, which nobody likes or comments on. I work on my costume in hopes that I'll go to San Diego Comic Con. But I don't really want anyone commenting on my stuff. Or seeing me. I feel as though I am already too exposed.

But I like and heart everything that Kasumi posts. I don't comment, because that would be crossing some kind of invisible line. But I heart away. Her cute new sweater. Her winning a science award. Her eating ice cream with the other kids from SEW. Her and Sophie holding hands.

I am hit with a wave of happiness because my girl Kasumi has found a girlfriend. And they look cute together. And I wish we could talk about it.

But when I see her latest picture up there, my heart freezes.

It's her and Sophie dressed up as Magnetic Pole and Lady Bird at the Team Tomorrow Fan Event.

They have their arms around each other like girlfriends. That part makes me happy. It's the fact that they are holding up Team Tomorrow swag bags. They are smiling big. The caption says, THE PERKS OF HAVING A CINEMATOGRAPHER DAD! A GOLDEN TICKET TO THE TEAM TOMORROW PREMIERE AT SAN DIEGO COMIC CON!

I am overcome with a wave of extreme jealousy. The worst green kind of envy. The worst, most horrible kind of fury. The worst, most ugly kind of thoughts.

That should be me, I think.

But of course it shouldn't. We aren't friends right now. Just because I am a bigger fan than either of them, it doesn't mean that I should be there. The fan event looks fun, and it looks like an anyone-could-have-fun kind of fun. It makes me miss Kasumi. Not for the event. For her.

My cursor hovers over the button. I hesitate. Then I heart it.

Good for her, I think.

And then I cry.

Twelve

Even Gargantua can't help me as I shrink.

I hover over my computer to try to get tickets for San Diego Comic Con and I fail. They are sold out within minutes. How are things ever going to get better?

They don't.

I sit there with my purple hair, depleted. And then later that morning, I'm in the middle of English class when I get the news. A monitor comes in and pulls me out of class and brings me to the office. Like I'm the one in trouble.

When I get to the office, I see that Grandma Jackie is there. I don't even hear her when she tells me that the verdict came in. My dad got a sentence of fifteen to twenty years. I just take my arms and push everything off of the desk and let it fly to the floor.

Gargantua also has a temper. It is her weakness and her strength.

My grandma tries to restrain me, but I shake her off, so a security guard is called in to hold my arms behind my back because I am writhing. The security guard is not holding me because I'm in trouble, it's to protect me. And in my fury, I know that they are not upset that I am upset. They are sad that I am so upset. They are saying things to me. "We'll get you counseling." "You can stay in here until the end of the day." "Do you want a glass of water? Or some juice?" "Is there anybody that we can pull out of class to sit with you?"

That's when I wail. There is no one to sit with me. I just have to sit with myself.

Grandma Jackie puts her arms around me and hugs me really tight.

I have no strength. I am weak. I need help. Even though Grandma Jackie is there with her arms all over me. Blocking me from other people so I have space. Standing in front of me when photographers try to take my picture when my grandma leads me to her car to take me home.

I am in shock.

There is so much paperwork to do when your parent goes to jail.

"Why haven't you filled out your questionnaire?" my grandmother asks me about the paperwork I have to fill out in order to visit my dad in jail.

"I keep meaning to," I say. "But schoolwork."

"It's been a few weeks now, and you still haven't visited your father, and you haven't done what you have to do in order to go," she says.

"I know," I say. "I wrote him."

"That's not the same."

"I'm engaging," I say.

She digs into her bag and pulls out another questionnaire.

"I got another one for you, in case you can't find yours," she says.

"I'll get to it," I say.

"Do it now," she says.

"I don't have a pen," I say.

She pulls out a pen and hands it to me.

"I can't go by myself," I say.

"That's not an excuse," she says. "I can take you."

"I have a lot of stuff I have to do," I say.

"This is important," she says.

"What's important to you and what's important to me are different," I say.

"Fill out the paperwork," she says, and then she walks away to go take care of other things on her to-do list.

I start to fill it out and then I find myself taking the ballpoint pen and scratching it and drawing loops and circles all over the page. I ruin the questionnaire. It is filled with dark blue streaks, and parts of the page are ripped.

When she comes back and sees what I've done, she's on the phone in a hot second.

"I'll handle it," she says as she starts googling and sending emails to people. And in no time at all, she's found me a therapist.

"I don't want to," I say.

"But you will anyway," Grandma Jackie says.

The only person I want to talk about things with, besides Kasumi, is Kirk. I muster up the courage to contact him. A last gasp from a girl who used to feel super and now feels like she's fading away in her lair.

Help me, Green Guarder, I text. *I am in need of a bloom.*

I don't hear anything back. And then a little voice that is Gargantua in me recalls one of her most famous lines when she thought that Green Guarder was dead forever and she'd lost him.

Be your own bloom.

Summer

SAN DIEGO
COMIC CON

One

When I finally go back to school and am sitting at lunch, staring at my uneaten banana, I'm surprised when someone taps me on the shoulder.

"Hey," says a kid that I don't know. "You're Edan, right?"

"Yeah," I say. I wonder if I'm going to get told to move. Or told that I'm terrible or told that I'm evil.

"I'm Juan," the boy says. "I'm Kirk's cousin."

"Oh," I say, squinting and now realizing that I recognize him. "Hi."

"Anyway," Juan says. "I thought you should know that Kirk's mom has had some surgery. He's been meaning to get back to you, about stuff, but the last couple of weeks were really intense for him."

"Oh," I say. "I'm so sorry."

"Yeah," Juan says. And then kind of presses his fists to his eyes. "It's really sad. Aunt Flora is the best."

I can tell that he's trying to hide some tears. And I have to admit that tears have sprung to my eyes. I put my arm out and touch his shoulder.

"I'm so sorry," I say.

"OK," he says. "I just had to pass along the message. I gotta go."

I think about it all. About how sad I am for Kirk. About how he is in pain. About how his pain affects me.

And it strikes me that even though my dad isn't dying, I have been grieving in a totally different way the loss of my dad.

"What are you going to do about it?" the therapist Grandma Jackie has organized for me asks when I'm sitting in her office. Talk therapy is helpful even though I don't always say everything.

"I don't know, I feel weird about everything," I say.

"That's normal," she says.

"I feel like I'm hurt because he didn't answer me and I was going through stuff, too. That silence killed me."

"But can you see that he wasn't being silent? Can you extend your view outside of yourself?"

"Yes," I say. "But I still feel weird."

"Life is all about feeling weird and awkward, and how you deal with it is the key," she says.

One thing that we talk about in therapy is making amends. How do people say *I'm sorry*? How do we hear *I'm sorry*?

I'm ready to say it even if the people I want to say

I'm sorry to don't want to hear it. So instead, I say it to the wind.

"I'm sorry," I say, and let the real, true repentance float out of me and over the city. "I'm sorry."

And there is power in that small thing. Knowing that I've said it and knowing that I mean it. And knowing that one day those I want to hear it will hear it.

There is so much power that we all have inside us.

When I leave the office, it takes me fifteen minutes to walk over. And during those fifteen minutes, I try to talk myself out of going. I am afraid that he's not going to want to see me.

But instead, when I ring the bell and he opens the door, he looks at me. And I look at him and in about two seconds we are hugging each other and crying.

This hug is one of those life hugs. Those hugs where you probably are hugging for an hour. Where you are melded with another person. Where you flow from you to them and back again. Where you are sure that each other's strength is passing from you to them and back again.

This is what it must feel like when Green Guarder and Gargantua help each other to come back to life.

After what seems like forever, we pull apart. Both of our faces are wet.

"I'm so sorry," we both say at the same time.

And it's like we're both sorry for everything. I'm sorry that Kirk's mom is not doing well. He's sorry that my dad is in jail.

We're both sorry to each other for having not been there for each other.

"Do you want to come in?" he asks as he takes my hand.

I nod and step through the door.

And suddenly, I know I'm in the right place. In the right story. With the right boy. With the right heart.

Two

I think nothing is going to be normal now that Dad is in jail.

But miracles do happen.

One day I come home from school and I hear something going on as I open the door. I can't imagine what it is, because I know that my mom has collapsed into herself more than she had before the verdict. But when I step inside, I see something surprising.

Mom is in the middle of the living room, hair washed, nice put-together outfit, and she's directing a bunch of men who are tagging furniture in the house.

"What's going on?" I ask. "Is everything getting re-possessed?"

She looks at me and I see a look that I haven't seen in her for a while.

"I'm taking care of business," she says. "We're going to be downsizing. We can't live here anymore, so I got us an apartment."

When you've had a year like mine, things slip. Grades slip. Friends slip. Life slips. When they do, if you're brave, really and truly brave, you ask for help.

"I need help," I say. "If I'm going to make it through this."

"Yes," my mom says. "Me, too."

I drop my bag off my shoulder to the floor. I can't believe what I'm hearing.

"I've been talking to the therapist and I'm seeing a lot of traps that I fell into," she says. "I don't want to be that person anymore."

"Me, neither," I say. "I feel like I've been so bad that no one can see the good."

"You haven't been bad," Mom says. "We've both been sideswiped."

I go and hug her. And it feels so good to be in her arms. Like I've gotten my mother back.

"Does Grandma Jackie know?"

"Yes," my mom says. "She cosigned the lease with me."

"Wow. When are we moving?"

"As soon as you're done with school."

"Am I going to have to change schools?" I ask.

"No," my mom says. "I found a spot right here in Los Feliz. A little higher than I wanted to pay, but I thought it was important to not disrupt you any more than you've already been disrupted."

I feel relieved. Then worried.

"How will we pay for it?" I ask the obvious question.

"I'm going to get a job," she says. "I put a call out to my old network of people and said I was looking to come back. I've got a couple of job interviews and lunches set up. Something will happen."

I know that she knows that they know what happened. But that's the thing about second chances. You don't have to be judged by what someone else has done. You can still be given a chance. My dad isn't my mom. She's her own person. Just like my dad isn't me.

"How can I help?" I ask.

"Figure out what you can sell," she says. "We're going to need something to start on."

"You got it," I say.

When starting over, sometimes you have to burn it all down.

I go to the task at hand with fervor. I am relentless. I strip it all down. I don't need anything.

Three

I'm sure I'll do poorly on my final exams because my academic year has been garbage. But the only test that I'm really hoping to ace is the test of my resolve to clear my name.

I gather up all of my evidence against Yuri and I sit outside the principal's office on the last day of school to plead my case.

"It's hard to tell," the principal says, looking over my stuff.

"I take full responsibility," I say. "For making a poor choice in Yuri as a treasurer and as a person in my life. But I don't think that I should be punished."

"Hmmmm," she says, clicking around on the club's social media page. "You all made these costumes?"

"Most of them," I say. "We try to make what we can. We repurpose pieces. We store-buy some. We commission some."

"I like the Silver Surfer," she says.

"You're a fan of comics?" I say, a little surprised.

"I was young once," she says. "And I'm still young at heart."

"Of course," I say. "One thing I was thinking, when my name is cleared . . ."

"If," she says, and then motions for me to continue.

"I was thinking that SEW could also do some charitable works. Show up at hospitals and libraries in costume."

She nods.

"You're not the only person insisting on an inquiry here," she says.

"I'm not?"

"You've got some friends who want this reopened," she says.

Her secretary comes in and announces the next meeting, and so I'm scooted out. Kirk is waiting for me.

"And?"

"And we'll see," I say. "But I feel like I did all I can."

"Just because you're not in SEW doesn't mean that you can't cosplay," Kirk says. "Like when you go to San Diego Comic Con."

"But I didn't get a badge," I say. "I tried but I didn't."

"Well, you maybe didn't get a regular badge," he says. "But if you want to come help your boyfriend work a booth at Comic Con, you could be an exhibitor."

"Really?" I say.

"Yeah," he says. "My mom gets too tired now. She wouldn't be able to do a full shift, but she doesn't want to miss San Diego. It might be her last. You'd really be helping me out."

"Yes. Yes. Yes," I say.

There are two things that he just said that make my heart leap. I am going to San Diego Comic Con. And Kirk is my boyfriend.

Four

My San Diego Comic Con pass arrives in the mail and it says EXHIBITOR. I have a job. I am going to go help Kirk and his family at their booth. I'll be sharing a room with his cousin Maria, who is also going to help out. I'm going to get paid by the hour for my booth shifts, but I'm going to have plenty of time to wander around. I can hardly believe it. I keep asking my mom over and over again to make sure it's true as she drives me to the train station.

"It's true," she says. "The Kupferman women are taking their lives back."

If I thought the comic book conventions I had gone to were overwhelming, they are nothing compared to San Diego. It's the Tuesday before the show; Kirk and his family have been here since yesterday driving down all the stuff. I'm here to help with the setup.

There is something beautiful about an empty convention center. At first the hall is empty, just tables and chairs and tape marks and boxes. But slowly over the day, the scaffolding of booths starts going up. And things start coming together and suddenly it's full of excitement and stuff.

On Wednesday evening, the doors open and the hall goes from empty to full in minutes flat.

"Oh my gosh," I say to Kirk.

"I know," he says. "It's like a wave."

"An endless wave of beautiful nerds," I say.

We do a brisk business and at one point I see Yuri, Phil, and Tze walking down our aisle. A part of me wants to hide behind the racks of clothing. But then I think better of it. Yuri can't touch me now. I have become Gargantuan. When he slows his stride by the booth, we lock eyes and I stare at him with every ounce of power that I have in me.

Yuri mutters something under his breath.

"Keep walking," I say. And there is some kind of power in me that makes him do just that.

When the hall closes, we exhaustedly go out for dinner. I can tell that Kirk feels down. He's worried about his mom. Being here is good for her, I can see that on her face. She loves this world. But it's hard on Kirk because her future is so uncertain.

"So guess what," I say, trying to change the vibe.

"What?" he asks. He's playing with my hand across the table.

"I found out through the girl in the booth next to ours that tomorrow night there is a secret premiere of *Team Tomorrow*."

"Well," Kirk says, "I heard about that, but you have to have a ticket from the fan event."

"But I found out that you can wait in a line all day for the chance to maybe get overflow seats."

"But we're working," he says.

"Maybe we could tag team," I say.

"How cool would it be to go to the premiere?" he says.

"Almost as cool as winning that cosplay contest," I say.

He flips open his notebook and shows me how we can possibly wait in shifts. "Let's see how we can figure it out."

"It's crazy," I say.

"I know," he says.

"But how can we not do it?" I ask.

"I know," he says. "What's the worst that can happen?"

"Disappointment," I say.

"We're not afraid of that, are we?"

"No," I say.

"Let's do it," I say.

five

Even though I get there super early, the line snakes around and I can't really tell if I'm in a good spot or really far back. To make things worse, it's some kind of random giveaway, so having a good place in line doesn't matter.

"Why are they doing that?" I ask no one in particular.

"They are afraid of scalpers and such," a dude behind us says. "They have a lot of trouble with non-fans and stuff."

"So you have to get a golden ticket," I say.

"Pretty much," the dude says. "But if you don't draw it on your first try, you can get back in line until they are all gone. But your plus-one has to be here if you draw the ticket."

I text Kirk the information. He responds with a million funny emojis.

KIRK: I'll make it work. Maria will cover for me.

It's hot outside. People have brought coolers and chairs. They are all pros when it comes to waiting in line. Kirk still hasn't arrived and it's almost my turn to pick a ticket. I look all around frantically.

The line inches closer, and two women a few people in front of me scream. They got a ticket. I watch with envy as they are both wristbanded.

Kirk still hasn't arrived and it's my turn. I stick my hand in the bucket and pull out a ticket.

"Sorry," the woman says. "You're not a winner. You can go line up again."

I'm half-glad that I didn't get it, because Kirk wasn't there and they are being very strict about it, and half-mad because I am sure that Kirk would have arrived soon. I trudge all the way to the back of the line, scanning for Kirk, who I don't see.

ME: *Where are you?*

As I'm walking to the now crazy-long end of the line, I hear my name.

"Edan?"

I stop and turn. It's Kasumi. She's with Sophie and they are both looking adorable in ruffle skirts and cat ears.

"Hey," I say. I want to stop because she said hello. But also I want to keep going because the line is getting longer.

"What's this line for?" she asks.

"*Team Tomorrow* screening," I say.

"Oh," Sophie says. "We got passes for it at the fan event."

I notice that Kasumi kind of nudges her and Sophie covers her mouth like she's realized she just stuck her foot in it.

"Comic Con is cool, right," Kasumi says.

I glance back over at the line.

"I'm going to go," I say. "I mean, it's so nice to see you. But I . . ."

"I get it," Kasumi says gently. Like a friend. "You want to get into the screening."

"Thanks," I say. Glad that she knows I'm not trying to be rude.

I scurry away and as I do, my phone pings. It's Kasumi.

Text me if you get in.

I get to the back of the line and am feeling totally hopeless. There is still no word from Kirk.

My phone pings. It's Kirk.

Get up to the front, it says.

I am hesitant to leave my place in line. But I take the chance. I walk briskly to the front of the line.

Kirk is standing there arguing with the woman with the bucket.

"See, she's here! She's here," Kirk says. "I'm sorry, I ran over here and then just got in the line and figured I'd try."

The woman looks at me with a glimmer of recognition.

"OK," she says. And then puts a wristband on Kirk and on me.

"We did it," I say.

"I fought to hold on to these wristbands like Green Guarder holding on to the time stream," he says.

"You are a fan," the woman says. "Glad this ticket went to someone who will appreciate it more than just being something free."

We go back to the convention hall to help finish selling things for the day. We have a plan to help out until the last minute and then run over to the Embarcadero to see the film. We don't really care that it means we'll get crappy seats. At least we'll be there.

Emboldened, I text Kasumi and tell her that Kirk and I got seats. She doesn't respond and I figure that maybe she was just being polite.

I've changed into my Gargantua costume and we're about to leave when Kirk's mom says, "Wait."

"We have to go," Kirk says.

"You can wait a few minutes," she says.

His mom hands me a bag and I open it. Inside is the dress from the mannequin. The beautiful one stitched with the Team Tomorrow fabric.

"For you," she says.

I hug it to myself. Loving it so much. Knowing that it is something that Kirk's mom made and that I will wear.

"Give me a second," I say. And even though I've waited all year to wear my Gargantua costume, I know that it's not the right thing to wear tonight. Kirk nods and I slip behind the dressing curtain and put it on. It needs a little altering, but it will do for now.

I step out and do a little twirl.

"You look really nice," Kirk says. I notice that he's changed out of his Green Guarder outfit into a button-down shirt with a suit coat that has the Team Tomorrow logo embroidered all over it. He sticks his elbow out and I loop my arm through his. It is nice to be dressed up and going to a premiere.

"Wait," his mom says before we head out. "Let me take a picture."

She pulls out her phone and takes our picture.

"Now you," I say. I take some pictures of Kirk and his mom and I know, the way that you know that a moment is important, that this will be a treasured memory.

There is a line to pick up our tickets at will call. The woman checks our wristband, makes a big mark on each, and then gives us an envelope.

"Great outfits," she says.

"His mom's company makes them," I say. "Booth G41."

"I'll come by. OK, there are box lunch tickets in there," she explains. "Also a ticket for a seat cushion. And your wristband serves as your swag bag ticket, so don't forget to pick it up after the movie."

"Are we late?" I ask.

"Oh, no," she says. "The actors are just getting to the red carpet, and there is a pre-show show. Actually, you should go line up with all the cosplayers and fans doing the fan red carpet. They're doing a contest."

"But we're not cosplaying," I say. "We're bounding."

She shrugs. "You still look great."

We have a choice, to try to scramble for seats in the bleachers or join the line of cosplayers who are being interviewed by an emcee as part of the preview. The whole thing is being projected onto the giant bubble screen.

"Is it OK if we go on the fan red carpet line?" I say. "I don't think it's going to change where we sit in the bleachers."

"You're reading my mind," Kirk says.

We stand in line with people taking pictures in front of the step and repeat and a bunch of the cosplayers who are trying to win the walk-on part for the contest. I compliment every single person.

"I never would have won this," I say to Kirk. "They all are such professionals here."

"Not all of them," he says, pointing to a little kid and a dude in a store-bought Lady Bird and Figment outfit.

After we take a picture or two, making Team Tomorrow poses, we try to ditch the line, but the emcee and camera crew stop us.

"Well, what do we have here?" he says. "A beautiful couple in Team Tomorrow fancy dress. Let's give a round of applause for on-point premiere fashion."

"Did you make these?" he asks, pointing the microphone at us. I am aware that we are being projected on the screen for the whole audience to see.

"His mom did," I say. "Booth G41."

"Really wonderful," the emcee says. "Now, I don't think this gives you an entry into the official contest, but how about we give this gorgeous couple a prize."

We look out and the whole crowd is applauding.

"Who's your favorite character?" he asks.

"Gargantua," I say.

"And Green Guarder," Kirk says.

He motions to a production assistant, who goes and grabs something from the side of the stage.

"Here is a collectible Green Guarder bus stop poster. Can't get one of these unless you steal it. And a limited edition Gargantua mask made from the mold of the mask that was actually used in the movie."

I hold the mask in my hand. It's heavy, sleek, and beautiful. It's better than a walk-on. It's a walk toward. It's a walk into.

The emcee moves on to the next people in line, and Kirk and I look at each other and let out a dorky squeal. I notice that there is a message on my phone, so when I get through, it's Kasumi.

Section B, tenth row. Come find me.

"It's Kasumi," I say. "Should we go see?"

Kirk nods and we head down toward the middle front.

"Kasumi!" I call, and she turns her head. She waves and then points to two seats behind her that are covered with two sweaters. Sophie leans back and says something to the person next to the seats, who comes and looks at us and waves.

I point to myself. To say, wait for me? For us?

271

Kasumi throws her hands in the air and makes a funny face, the kind she always makes that makes me laugh. And waves and points to the seats again. Like she's my friend. Like she wants me to join her.

Kirk and I make our way down the row and get to the seats. Kasumi is standing up.

"Ahhhhhhhh!" Kasumi says. "You looked so cool up there!"

"Isn't this reserved?" I say.

She shrugs.

"I pulled some strings," she says. "We got in early and I just figured it would be OK."

She's standing up now. And we're looking at each other. And sometimes you know that an action is really a "let's just move forward from this moment." And I know that we are back.

I pull her in for a hug.

We can stand on a stage. Bright lights. Costumes. Dazzle everywhere. But nothing beats being in a real duo, doing heroic things. Or forming your own team.

That's what my real-life Team Tomorrow is all about.

"Thank you," I say. "This is amazing."

"There's going to be a live orchestra playing the soundtrack," Sophie says. "And there's ice cream. I was going to go get some. Do you want chocolate or vanilla?"

"Chocolate," I say.

"You look nice," Kasumi says. "That's a great dress."

"My mom made it," Kirk says.

"She's got gorgeously geeky stuff," I say. "You should come by the booth tomorrow when I'm working, Kasumi."

Kirk opens up our lunch boxes and makes a little spread out of the seat cushion while I keep talking with Kasumi.

"Just so you know," Kasumi says. "We wrote a petition to look into the dues discrepancy."

"I hoped that was you," I say. "I gave all the info I have to the principal."

"I'm sure it will be sorted out. I know that it wasn't you. I was just so mad."

"I know," I say. "I'm sorry. I should have told you what was going on with me. I just didn't know how to tell you."

"It's hard to figure out so many things," Kasumi says. "But it's not hard to figure out that you and I are friends."

"I'm hoping that I can rejoin SEW in the fall," I say. "And I've got some great ideas about volunteer work that we can do."

I lay out my plan about visiting kids in the hospital and doing school visits. "I love it!" she says.

I sit down and eat my sandwich and hold hands with Kirk and watch the pre-show. The cast and crew come out and give little speeches about *Team Tomorrow*.

Everything is about to begin.

The lights come down. The orchestra conductor raises his baton. The music starts. The title comes up.

I have goose bumps all over.

Acknowledgments

Thank you to my wonderful literary champions, my agent Kirby Kim, editor Nancy Mercado, David Levithan, and Scholastic Press.

Thank you to every person I ever nerded out with about something. Like my brother. And Steve Salardino. And the Shamers. And all my friends. And all nerdy girls everywhere.

I would like to acknowledge here and now that if you think you are a nerd or geek or dork, you are and you are a real one. Your enthusiasm shines the way and I love it.

About the Author

Cecil Castellucci is the author of numerous books and graphic novels for young adults including *Boy Proof, The Plain Janes, First Day on Earth, The Year of the Beasts, Tin Star,* and *Soupy Leaves Home*. In 2015 her childhood dream came true when she co-authored *Moving Target: A Princess Leia Adventure in Advance of Star Wars: The Force Awakens*. Other nerdy bucket list characters she's written comics for are Wonder Woman, Aquaman and Mera, the cast of Deep Space Nine, and rebooting the character of Rac Shade in the ongoing series Shade, The Changing Girl. Her first comic book boyfriend at age four was Batman. She went to her first comic book convention at age eleven, where she cosplayed Jessica Six from *Logan's Run*. She had a band called Nerdy Girl in the mid-nineties and in 1999 she lived in a tent on Hollywood Boulevard for six weeks to wait for tickets for *Star Wars: Episode I*. She is an honorary member of the 501st Legion. She is very nerdy and lives in Los Angeles.